B.E.S.T.

Jenn Sadai

AOS Publishing, 2024

ISBN: 978-1-990496-24-0

Cover Design: Kim Teves

Visit AOS Publishing's website:
www.aospublishing.com

PREFACE

B.E.S.T. is a fictional story that I wish could become factual, though I must admit is pure fantasy. My mind struggles to fathom a successful democratic society free from violence and inequality. It's a far-fetched dream, carefully crafted to offer hope to a world that is slowly breaking apart.

And isn't hope what we need?

We're destroying the environment, polluting the air, and tearing down trees to put up commercial greed machines. The ecosystem is off kilter; irresponsible human intervention is spinning Mother Nature into unprecedented storms and chaos. Resources are dwindling and rage is rising. The daily news is bleak and our bright future is fading.

I can't deny our reality.

In desperate times, hope that change is truly possible is the only way to motivate people to put in the work to make the necessary changes. We need to first believe that a world free from violence could actually work and a thriving utopia could possibly one day exist, otherwise, why even try? We must aim higher than reality and then celebrate every improvement made along the way.

Realistically, I do not expect that this book will change the world, but that doesn't stop me from hoping it will.

Sincerely,
Jenn Sadai

B.E.S.T.

What About Us?

When all hope is lost, wouldn't any idea sound like a good plan, at least in theory? Sometimes a Hail Mary pass is the only shot you've got. You close your eyes, give it everything you can, and pray for the best possible outcome. It's not a matter of win or lose, it's do or die, everything teetering on the line.

Mother Earth was helpless, sinking on her deathbed and pleading for the environmental abuse to cease. Most people assumed attempting to revive Her was futile and succumbed to the chaos overwhelming everyday life. No one with any power was willing to make any real sacrifices and hopelessness consumed all those who believed they were powerless.

A sensation of doom suffocated anyone who tried to improve the situation; it was too grand of a task for any one person to consider tackling. It would take the collective efforts of hundreds, probably thousands, of passionate people to stop the destruction and rebalance the earth, environmentally and politically.

Someone had to gather enough people and present a plan solid enough to contradict the overwhelming belief that saving the planet had become a lost cause. The world needed one person with enough hope and determination to redirect the world back on the right path, before it was lost for good.

"Good morning, Arturo." The Colonel stood up to greet her guest, who gently knocked on the open steel door, advising her of his presence.

"Good morning, Colonel Harrison. Is there anything I may help you with today?" The slender man's eagerness beamed through his smooth white teeth.

"Yes, if you don't mind. Please ask Kali, Calvin, and Ariel to stop by my office before they leave for the day. Can you also ask Dawna to send me the cost estimates for building the new solar farm? And please accept the invite from Sarah to play tennis next week." Still standing at her desk, Colonel Amica Harrison swiped away each alert from the virtual screen projected from her wristband, automatically transferring the task to her assistant.

"I will take care of this right away. Is there anything else?" Arturo clicked each alert, accepting the task from his leader and long-time friend.

"Thank you, Sir. That's all I truly need." Colonel Harrison gave her assistant a curt nod of appreciation before sitting back down at her understated, streamlined workstation. At first glance, you could only see a mid-sized black table with a leather office chair on one side and two antique-style guest chairs poised with their backs to the entrance.

One swipe of her slender finger unlocked a small control panel hidden within the center of the wall. Sensitive sensors discreetly disguised in the faux wood confirmed it was the Colonel's fingerprint, however that was only the first security step. Amica still had to enter a ten digit password, which triggered the retina scanner to appear a foot above the digital panel. A sliding door opened, took a quick scan of her piercing blue eyes, and confirmed that it was in fact Amica Harrison, Senior Colonel of B.E.S.T. The physical and financial security of millions of people under her leadership was held within her personal batcave.

B.E.S.T. was the acronym given to the project Colonel Harrison, Commander Ying, Prime Minister Cortez, Supreme Minister Jordynna Forte, Doctor Gia Romano, Doctor Andrameda Martin, Doctor Ariel Sinclair, Kali Robbins, and environmental expert Dawna Marchand created to save the world four years prior. Over time, it took on the name of the new utopia they built, as it was, simply, the BEST place to live.

Balance, Equity, Stability, Teamwork.

Those were the four pillars required to right-side the earth after mankind slowly spun it off its axis. Balance to restore the environment, equity to resolve socio-economic injustices, laws and practices to maintain stability, and of course teamwork. Every member of the new world would be a part of both the work and the rewards. The world had to be rebuilt from the ground up, the ecosystem revived back to the state it was in before greed and corruption took over. Mankind had to give the earth the B.E.S.T. care possible if there was any hope to save it.

It was the worst of humanity that caused the deadly turmoil; only the best would reverse it.

The Great American War began in 2030 and was a civil war fought over how the country should be run. Climate crisis activists were up against climate change deniers. Immigration supporters and those who felt foreigners were ruining the country. People believing in women's right to an abortion versus those obsessed with the right to life. Their views were polar opposites and neither side would give up what mattered most to them. Gun rights was the immovable line.

When war broke out, the Southern Conservatives began building walls and bunkers throughout each city, blocking themselves off from those that did not share the same political and religious views. The United Resistors Coalition protested the segregation relentlessly, only causing tensions to escalate.

Since their government had already lost all credibility due to distrust in their election process and wild propaganda-based campaigns, the new Democratic administration was under relentless attacks. There was a never-ending stream of slanderous campaigns pouring out from both sides and no governing body willing to interfere with the daily battles popping up on every street corner.

Every death and mass shooting was sensationalized in the mainstream media, pushing fear to rise on both sides. Americans started carrying weapons everywhere they went for protection. Hospitals and graveyards were physically overflowing with patients who had been injured or killed as the result of opposing political beliefs. Prisons and courthouses were bursting at the seams and murderers were walking free while they waited years for trial dates that never got scheduled.

Wicked storms plaguing the Southern borders added desperation to the chaos. Florida started to noticeably shrink in the winter of 2026, and was almost completely underwater before the war began. The shorelines of Louisiana and Texas, as well as most of Mexico, sank underwater, forcing Southerners and Mexican asylum-seekers to overtake property further inland. Since the frequency and destructiveness of the storms increased, natural resources and basic necessities were in short supply. Overcrowding and food rationing fueled the madness.

The United States of America was the first country to break apart from the inside, but it didn't take long for the anger and violence to spread across the world. Domestic war broke out in Russia, as civilians blamed government propaganda on the loss of hundreds of thousands of soldiers fighting in Ukraine. Small scale protests and internal upheaval ramped up in Syria, Iran, Afghanistan, and the European Union.

Eager to take advantage of conflict spreading globally and establish their power, North Korea was the first country to set off nuclear weapons of mass destruction. The intended target was South Korea, but the fallout showered over Japan, parts of China, and most of the surrounding ocean. China retaliates against North Korea in full-scale war and inadvertently kills a group of soldiers stationed along the Russian border. Russia, eager to turn their internal conflict outward, bombs China and re-engages war in Ukraine.

War ignited everywhere and missiles started to fly daily through the night sky in every direction. Most of Europe, Saudi Arabia, Iraq, Israel, and even the United States, temporarily interrupted their raging civil battles to flex their military muscle in a massive global pissing contest. Tanks blazing and sporadic explosions left carnage and rubble scattered through major cities like discarded hoagie wrappers strewn in a New York alley.

All of Asia was inhabitable within a matter of months. Russia had been virtually wiped off the map as well. Most of the countries in the European Union had only thousands, if not hundreds of people left, scrambling to survive. Canada, Australia, Africa, and the majority of South America were the only areas untouched by missiles or nuclear bombs.

War ruled humanity's reality across the globe.

Mother Nature raged in response. Rising water wiped out every island in the Caribbean, parts of Northern Canada and Iceland, all of Greenland, the Philippines, New Zealand, and Madagascar. Millions of people who were unable to relocate before the storms hit were rotting among the decades of plastic suffocating every major body of water.

While wars were breaking out all over the world, Colonel Harrison was developing a hydro-powered filtration system for a prominent environmental research company that had the potential to be scaled large enough to sweep the ocean free from debris in a few short days. It was a massive project; she recruited two co-workers, Dawna Marchand and Kali Robbins, to join the efforts. Funding was limited, since most political leaders had given up on saving the world. Doomsday felt too soon to fathom any hope of creating lasting, worthwhile change.

The filtration system was just the beginning, and new ideas about how to combat the environmental and political problems plaguing the world kept popping up in her head. Amica began mapping out an extensive plan that far exceeded the scope of merely cleaning the waterways. The only real issue was that it would take an army to pull off her elaborate concept successfully.

It sounded like a far-fetched, delusional idea, so the first time Amica had the courage to share it out loud did involve a little bravery-inducing THC. Maybe it wouldn't sound quite as crazy if everyone had a bit of a buzz going into the unconventional conversation.

Amica's lifelong friend, Royelle, whipped up a batch of her best cannabis, chocolate, walnut brownies for a friendly gathering in the Spring of 2041. The rare treat was presented on a teal blue glass platter to the four women gathered in Amica and Royelle's quaint country cabin.

"These are special brownies, with something extra to help us prepare mentally for doomsday." The leggy Nordic beauty placed the treats on a hand-carved wooden patio table, centered between Amica and Dawna.

Kali's eyes lit up as she grabbed one, devouring the gooey dessert in a matter of bites. Amica and Dawna carefully selected theirs, then picked at them slowly. Royelle made sure to test the batch prior to serving, but still snuck one more to enjoy with her dear friends.

"Oh my God, that was good, Royelle. Will it be too much if I have another?" Kali pondered out as she scooped another one..

"Be too much for what? It's not like we have anywhere we need to be. Haven't you noticed it's a ghost town anywhere you go these days? There is no one around to judge you if you get a little silly." Royelle was enthusiastically licking chocolate from her fingers as she reassured her friend.

"You know we don't judge!" Amica chimed in with a big grin.

"True dat." Dawna lifted her sour soda water into the air with vigor.

"Our days are numbered, might as well enjoy them!" Kali cheered before scooping a second treat from the tray.

"Yeah, yeah, the world is ending. Have we really given up?" Amica stared into her friends, penetrating their hearts with her puppy dog eyes.

"Hey, no one wants to say 'fuck it' and just give up. However, no one in government is doing anything to change things, why should we? What's the point of trying to clean the oceans if the entire world is at war?" Kali clapped back as she leaned back in her bright pink zero-gravity chair.

"Superman couldn't save this shithole from sinking. No one cares enough to change anything." Dawna stated matter-of-factly.

"What about us?" Amica asked with the utmost sincerity.

"What about us, what?" Dawna responded, each word dripping with doubt.

"What about us changing things? We care about this world." Amica asked again.

"Eat another brownie, crazy chick." Royelle was sitting next to Amica, and reached her arm around to pull her in close. She whispered with a smile: "Always a dreamer, eh?"

"Always." Amica stood up from the patio bench and began pacing around her friends, cracking her knuckles nervously. "Dreams give us hope, and couldn't we all use a little more hope right now?"

"I hope things can get better, and I won't give up. It's just hard to believe things will ever actually get better." Dawna said sincerely.

"I believe there is a way to fix everything, and *we* can be the ones to create real change. Hear me out, ladies. I've given this some real thought and have an actual solution." Amica inhaled deeply, pausing to gather the thoughts and confidence before laying out the extensive details. As she spoke, Kali sat back upright; Dawna and Royelle leaned in, hanging on her every word. No one laughed and her friends were nodding in agreement by the end.

Dawna and Kali vouched for the environmental aspect of Amica's complex agenda. Their current project involved utilizing recycled plastic and used tires from landfills, which could be obtained at almost zero cost. Building the larger device would be difficult and would require a sizable team, but it was one of the few feasible theories the scientific world had yet to try.

The once-shy Amica Harrison now had her small team buzzing with hope and brownies, ready to take real action. They knew they would need a lot of help to pull it off, so the following day, the four women reached out to every affluent and educated friend that they thought would be willing to participate. It was a simple enough inquiry to start, though it had many pending plans hiding within.

Ideas Into Action

The first official meeting of B.E.S.T. took place on June nineteenth, 2041 at nine am in Colonel Amica Harrison's cozy cabin in Smiths Falls, Ontario, Canada. The high-tech security the Colonel currently had in her office/batcave wasn't necessary until several years later. The new world was merely a concept that ran on a continuous loop in her mind. When the team kicked things off in 2041, Amica couldn't be certain her ideas were plausible, let alone effective. She was desperate for feedback outside of her immediate circle.

Nine of the brightest minds on the planet arrived at the wood cabin precisely on time, eager to tackle the rapid destruction of the very ground they stood on. It was not the Colonel's intention to have only women at the table, but not one of the male leaders she contacted was able to attend the initial meeting.

Colonel Harrison had prepared a compelling argument and a summary of the plan to clearly outline the purpose for their gathering. Although it was only a small group of nine women, and Amica had once commanded hundreds, her palms were damp and her fingers trembled. She only had one chance to inspire real action. Inhale, exhale and let the words flow, she recited the mantra internally until the moment her mouth opened in front of them.

"Thank you sincerely for showing up today. My colleagues and I need your help to brainstorm a realistic way to rebalance our broken world. We have ample ideas that will create real change, but we need help with financing and execution. If we work together, I'm confident we can rebuild a functioning society before the ground around us sinks too far to save." Amica's voice was clear and confident, in spite of her shaky hands.

"Kali Robbins, Dawna Marchand, and myself have spent the last few years developing a hydro-powered filtration system that will purge ninety to ninety-five percent of the debris currently suffocating our oceans. We know it will work and can eventually be scaled to cover a significantly larger surface space. Unfortunately, we lack the funding, manpower, and supplementary programs to truly test its capabilities."

A loud sigh escaped from one of their guests; another was chewing on her fingernail noisily. No one was making eye contact with her. Amica took a deep breath and continued with her planned speech.

"We tried to convince the remaining Canadian government that it was worth the investment, but there's no one left that we can ask. We currently don't have a Prime Minister and no one in Parliament is showing up to work. The people in power stopped looking for solutions; they decided that any hope for a viable future has been lost." Heads were nodding slowly as she spoke, eyes glazed over as they listened to their sad, shared reality .

Hope had been in short supply for decades.

Faith in politicians was non-existent. It wasn't until the world was facing undeniable and permanent extinction that world leaders finally accepted there was an urgent demand for dramatic policy changes. Corporate greed and corruption were forced to take a backseat to strict and restrictive environmental policies, regardless of their popularity.

For more than half of the world, the new, more conscientious rules, were too late or loosely enforced to be effective. Every body of water was rotted by debris and air quality was literally poisonous in heavily-populated North American and Asian cities. Numerous cities, as well as a few countries, had been permanently destroyed by nuclear blasts. Antarctica was underwater, large ice caps melted into the overflowing oceans, and summer temperatures scorched the leaves on taller trees to a rich autumn brown.

The world population was on a thirty-year decline and was estimated to be approximately half of what it used to be at the turn of the twenty-first century. The most current population assessment was conducted in 2038 and it determined there were fewer than three billion people living on earth.

A few years later, the majority of those people were malnutritioned vagrants stealing to survive. Devastation accelerated when a series of wicked viruses and variants wiped out six percent of the world population between 2020 and 2029. It bankrupted more than a billion people worldwide, the majority of whom lived in the United States.

The battle against the invisible killer that began with solidarity and selflessness ended in blame and self-preservation at all costs. Heroes were ostracized for being potential carriers and essential protection was auctioned off to the highest bidder. Human connection suffered the greatest blow, as one world leader after another traded the resurgence of the economy over the prevention of further deaths.

The first global strategy for dealing with the pandemic was to separate people from one another to stop the spread: 'social distancing.' It was a necessary step that possibly saved the world from faster extinction, however it led to unprecedented violence at a moment in history when the world desperately needed to heal.

Human life was no longer considered priceless.

Baby Boomers told stories of panicking in 1999 over the eve of the new millennium, aka Y2K, when experts were predicting that doomsday was imminent. People spent a significant amount of money and resources preparing for technological devastation, and fortunately their fears were unfounded. Nothing life-altering occurred, leaving some with a bitterness for proactive planning. Their disregard for global warnings was supported by their parent's childhood tales of going through the similar costly preparation building bomb shelters for a nuclear attack that failed to ever come to fruition

When Al Gore's highly-publicized global warming warnings didn't happen as quickly as predicted, many were convinced another false flag was being waved. World leaders downplayed the potential chaos and business continued as normal. Generation X gained influence and stepped into power positions at the start of the new millennium, however they were too busy chasing their dreams and pushing back against the workaholic expectations their parents established to worry over anything that was directly impacting their daily lives.

Schooling in the twenty-first century finally focused on the dangers of permanently destroying ecosystems and rapidly-shrinking resources, creating an awareness that had been intentionally hidden prior. Corporations and government bodies continued to counter the facts being taught, as a way to avoid the expense of implementing necessary changes.

By the time more progressive young minds rose into power, wicked storms were already stripping the shorelines and flooding major cities. Chunks of the coastlines were hidden below sea level in the heavily-polluted oceans. Policies were eventually put into place to slow down the damage, however they were almost impossible to enforce when the future of the environment had to take a backseat to the insanity of World War Three.

The gradual slide into climatic catastrophe and apocalyptic world war sped up drastically when the United States was sliced along its belly during the 2030 war between the Southern Conservatives and the United Resistor Coalition. The country's racist history had been brewing in dark alleys and prison cells ever since Dr. Martin Luther King Jr. shone a light on the systemic injustices discrimination was causing over seventy-five years ago.

The illusion of equality was present on the surface until Donald J. Trump was elected President of the United States in 2016, immediately after the first Black President, Barack Obama, finished his second term. Trump's team used white fears and prejudices to rile an angry base, unwilling to lose their privilege without a fight.

For four years, racist remarks and discriminatory policies were suddenly acceptable at the highest level. White supremacists became increasingly emboldened and worshiped the 'non-politician' who had the power to save them from their racist fears. It wasn't only the Black Lives Matter movement that had white people concerned for their privilege; immigrants of all races were depicted as threats. White pride masked as national pride, making America great again.

A slight majority of the population saw the danger on the horizon and advocated obsessively to expose the truth. That was how the Democratic party was able to defeat Trump in 2020, and then eventually gained control of the House, Senate, and Presidency. Their aggressive stances on controversial subjects unfortunately didn't capture the hearts of half their countrymen.

Donald Trump didn't go out quietly, and new conspiracies of a stolen election further ignited his base. One side stewing over losing their beloved leader, while the other side's overly-eager agenda to change the toxic culture led to the only possible outcome: greater friction. The inevitable war between the Alt-Right and the Far Left finally broke out in the Democrats' third term in power, after the laws were changed to prohibit automatic assault weapons.

Former Vice President, Kamala Harris, won the Presidency in the 2028 election and was able to pass a bill forcing gun owners to relinquish their automatic weapons. AK-47 and AR-15 enthusiasts, funded by the National Rifle Association, used their high-powered weapons to defend their right to bear arms with brute force. Peaceful protests ignited into gun-blazing rallies.

Civil war quickly ensued and every American felt they had no choice other than to pick a side. Officially, the war lasted until October nineteenth, 2037, when both sides reluctantly agreed that the United States of America as a whole could not be amicably reunited.

Young Activist and Entrepreneur, Graycee Mojica, was elected President of the Northern State Community, and Donald Trump Junior was rewarded with the title of President for the New United Republic. They originally agreed that N.U.R. would only consist of seven choice states, located along the South-East border.

The two inexperienced politicians were merely figureheads; both developing countries were scattered with angry citizens, reckless rebels, and deadly thieves who refused to be governed. The political divide was escalating in every city, as residents refused to move from their homes, even if they preferred the policies on the opposing side of this new imaginary border. Trump Junior was continuously employing his gun-toting army to claim new States in the name of N.U.R.

Over the course of the seven-year Civil War, nearly twenty million Americans lost their lives, plus approximately fifty-two hundred asylum seekers who were brutally murdered when a white terrorist group left vans full of pipe bombs at several overpopulated immigration detention centers.

The internal war in the United States inspired similar rebellions in several other countries and by the summer of 2039, more than half the world's population had been blown up on battlefields, while the other half was killing in the name of survival. All of this death occurred as the planet itself teetered on the brink of environmental extinction.

The Colonel lived through the same heartbreaking history that sucked the hope from the souls of the strong women in front of her. Convincing anyone that our dying world could be saved wouldn't be easy, despite the alternative outcome being absolutely unimaginable.

Selling Hope

Colonel Harrison's planned speech was interrupted when Doctor Martin slowly raised her hand.

"If the government has lost hope and is unwilling to help, how can we realistically hope to cause real change? Experts have said the world is too far gone to make a difference now," the Doctor stood up and stated with genuine concern.

It was a fair question: one she had prepared to answer. Amica slowly scanned each of the faces in front of her. She saw enough kind eyes and smiles in the small crowd for her to continue, in spite of the obvious skepticism clouding the room.

"Well, I strongly disagree with anyone who thinks the only answer is giving up. And you being here today shows me that you haven't lost hope, either. We can still turn things around if everyone works together. Regardless of how tough any situation might feel when you're in the thick of it, there is always hope things can and will get better.

"We need your help in raising funds, recruiting team members, and brainstorming ways to reduce the political turmoil, so our efforts are worthwhile. I want to hear your ideas for complementary programs to reverse the damage that is surrounding us. Our world needs a miracle and this fierce group in front of me may just be the only hope mankind has left."

In spite of her stoic demeanor, the direness and urgency in her words was undeniable. Every woman in the room understood the gravity of the situation. They traveled from various ends of what remained of the earth, because it was the first time in years someone suggested the planet could be saved.

To emphasize their collective concerns, the muscular, formidable former military leader allowed a drawn-out sigh to pour from her lips before proceeding with her agenda. Colonel Harrison wore her emotions like the soft smile on her cheeks, always forced, tight, and intentional.

"Before we get too deep into the details of my plan, I'd like to break into teams of three, to brainstorm recruitment strategies, identify challenges, and discuss how we can turn these ideas into action.

"I'm an environmental engineer and retired Colonel in the Canadian Armed Forces. My group will delve into the immediate steps that need to be taken to balance the world, both environmentally and politically. The world is not worth saving if we can't put an end to the destructive wars," Amica continued her rehearsed speech on autopilot.

"Standing next to me is Kali Robbins; she was EPC Global's Public Relations & Marketing Specialist for the past four years. Her experience includes global promotional campaigns, mass fundraising, and large event-planning. We will need to convince large-scale donors that the world can be saved, so they will stop wasting every cent under the assumption our days are numbered. We also need to trade power for protection with remaining world leaders. Kali's group will focus on generating funds and creating a foundation for a more equitable society.

"On my left is Dawna Marchand, an expert on our current climate crisis and the environmental impacts it has created. For now, her team's focus will be on recruitment and how to make our efforts sustainable. There's no point in draining the lakes and ocean of sewage if the sludge is only going to reappear in a year. We need sustainable policies and practices, which her team will develop and implement.

"I'm well-aware of the caliber of women in front of me and how most of you will be an asset to any team you choose to join. I want you to be passionate about the team you pick, so please speak up if there is a team you feel that you could benefit the most. Does anyone have a particular preference or a specialty?"

Colonel Harrison's military experience taught her that sharing power was far more productive than dictating tasks. Her instincts were right, as each woman volunteered, one by one, for the taskforce they were most excited or qualified to work on. The energy in the room rose as each woman staked her claim.

"If no one else objects, I would like to work on Kali's team. The New Republic government will no longer fund any medical supplies, so I'm often pleading with large companies to donate their inventory at a fraction of what it's worth. I also have a few diplomatic connections through Doctors Without Borders that could be beneficial." Doctor Andrameda Martin was the first one to voice her preference.

"As the Prime Minister of Australia, I am best suited for either Kali's or your team." Prime Minister Felicia Cortez quickly followed suit. "Our country still has resources and good people that would be interested in helping."

"I'm relieved to hear you say that, as I would like to work with you on the most hazardous obstacle we face. You're an essential part of my plan to end the violence, but I'd prefer to save that discussion for a later time. For today, you can help Kali with fundraising, and then I'll need you to go home and gather everything you can," The Colonel vaguely explained and Prime Minister Cortez nodded in agreement.

A petite woman in her forties, Commander Mei Ying of the former Beijing army, was the next woman to speak up. "I would like to work with you, Colonel. I already have a few suggestions regarding what will be necessary for us to revive humanity. I've been wracking my brain over this same nightmare for years. Nearly everyone I knew was either killed on impact or permanently disabled by the NK35 blast. A peace treaty must be an essential part of the earth's recovery. We cannot save the world if it's at constant war with itself."

"I agree, and would also love to be on your team. I believe those who are willing to work hard and make sacrifices to rebuild our world deserve a safe space, free from the toxicity, violence, corruption, and chaos that is dominating our world. We need to regroup somewhere, but where? I fear the European Union has no land left worth saving." Supreme Minister Forte's words were followed by a unanimous loud exhale, resonating deeply within each woman around the rectangular, hardwood table.

Although the millions of lives lost to war, unprecedented storms, and rising oceans were most definitely the greatest tragedy of Europe's quick demise, the permanent loss of history and culture felt almost just as heartbreaking. When the top half of the Eiffel Tower slowly sunk into the *port de suffren*, people risked their lives, and several died, trying to preserve nuts and bolts from the structure. The suicide rate throughout the European Union skyrocketed after the Colosseum in Rome collapsed.

Earth was self-imploding.

"I would be grateful to have both of you on my team, Supreme Minister Forte and Commander Ying. If no one has a better suggestion, my plan is to rebuild right here, within the heart of Canada. I think the perimeter should surround the Great Lakes and include a portion of the Northern State Community," Colonel Harrison replied while her assistant Arturo typed notes outlining the organization of the team members.

"Are you planning on excluding the New United Republicans from the new world we are building?" Doctor Martin instantly shot up to her feet as the only member of N.U.R. in attendance. Her hazel eyes pressed deeper into the Colonel with each word. Amica met her gaze and refused to flinch.

"There's a systematic method that I believe we can use that will separate the New United Republic population into two categories: those who can benefit our utopia and those who will destroy it. In order for this strategy to work, the details must be kept highly classified. Unfortunately I'm unable to discuss it until I determine who the members of that team will be." As the Colonel calmly explained her position, Doctor Martin slowly sank back into her chair, allowing a deflated sigh to escape her.

With a quick glance at the org. chart on the screen to her left, Amica continued, "That leaves Doctor Romano and Doctor Sinclair. Would you feel confident working with Dawna on a program to revive our Great Lakes and ensure the stability of any environmental improvements we make?"

"I'm willing to do whatever it takes to give mankind a chance of surviving another decade." A tall woman with thick black curls leaped from her seat to proclaim her willingness. Gia was genuinely excited to be around other people who still had hope for the future. She hadn't stopped grinning since she walked through the door.

"Same here. Whatever you need. There are ways to sustain our progress, but I believe it involves going back to our roots. We need to tend the land, focus on farming and soil preservation. I worked for Big Pharma for almost a decade before realizing its solutions were often more toxic than the illness it was trying to cure. Mother Nature has the answers," Doctor Ariel Sinclair added from her seat. The physically striking woman with brilliant blue eyes had her MD and then went on to obtain a doctorate in environmental health sciences.

"Perfect! Greed and chemicals have brought us to this point in history. Giving back and trusting nature is the core of our solution for a sustainable future." An almost undetectable glance in the direction of her assistant and the graph on the screen was updated to show the three groups summarized by their main focus and the members who volunteered for each.

"Someone has to save this world or it's game over. Through balance, equity, stability, and, of course, teamwork, we will do our best to become the heroes earth so desperately needs." She pumped both fists in the area instinctually, energized at the thought of her plans becoming possible.

The Colonel's atypical enthusiasm sparked a roar in the room; Arturo and the eight other women stood, clapping in support. Amica waited, standing firmly at attention, for the ladies to settle back down before proceeding with her plan. "Time is critical, so I'd appreciate it if we could begin immediately. We'll break into three groups and focus today's efforts on contacting potential team members and donors. Arturo will move between the groups to keep us organized"

The women nodded eagerly in agreement. The teams divided into various rooms throughout the cabin and began jotting down potential names, sending emails, making phone calls and desperately trying to sell the idea that earth was not a lost cause. Royelle, who spent most of the meeting baking in the kitchen, gave each group of three a small basket with mini maple sodas, sugared apple slices, dried mangoes, oatmeal cookies, and bite-sized protein balls.

Progress was minimal and they were only able to convince a few close friends or family members. Anyone who once had prominent careers in the government, law enforcement, or the military wouldn't even entertain the conversation. Every thirty or forty minutes, the individual groups of three would put down their phones to see if anyone had found an effective way to spark more interest.

"A former New York City Chief of Police told me to go fuck myself, so I don't think he wants to help." Doctor Martin rolled her eyes, slowly shaking her head in frustration. Police departments were the first to fall apart during the war. If they didn't shoot first, they were killed by rebels and rioters. If they did shoot first, they were demonized by the media. Damned if they do and damned if they don't; their badges one by one were tossed into the trash.

"I've called the most educated and compassionate people I know and none are interested in volunteering their time or contributing any money. I understand some of them are saving lives for practically nothing right now, but all of their efforts will be worthless if the earth sinks to the bottom of the ocean. I wish I could make them understand the urgency," Ariel vented loudly into the air, after a particularly frustrating debate with an affluent surgeon who cut her off twice before she could even share her pitch.

"Have you tried saying exactly that?" Doctor Romano replied, who was also having little success convincing the doctors she knew from the former Henry Ford and Mount Sinai Hospitals that the world could possibly be saved. Most of them were no longer practicing medicine, and several had turned to hardcore drugs and alcohol to cope with trauma they experienced during the past three pandemics. Medical professionals were in as short of a supply as everything else that held value, including hope.

"I've said exactly that and they're still not interested." The twenty-two-year-old doctor had been rapidly pacing the narrow, fourteen-foot-long hallway for over twenty minutes as she scrolled through every contact on her phone. "I understand they are currently working around the clock for very little money. That is precisely why they should invest in a plausible solution. World order needs to be restored, so they can be fairly compensated again."

The same struggles were echoing from the other side of the room.

"Why is it this hard to convince people that the earth is worth saving? Most of my contacts won't even respond to my message alerts or connect requests," Supreme Minister Jordynna Forte vented after making over twenty unsuccessful attempts. "Now that over half the country has dipped below the shoreline and the rest is being ravaged by civilian wars, no one wants to work in government or participate in any form of social services. Truthfully, most of our citizens don't want to work, period."

The European Union created the Supreme Minister position after the assassination of King William in 2037. The once-mighty British monarchy was brought down in a single day by hundreds of rebels armed with long knives and automatic weapons. Thousands of protestors stormed the guards at Buckingham Palace, guns blazing in every direction. The only surviving princess was dragged outside and tossed into the street like trash. Random people took over possession of the Palace, which instantly transformed into a never-ending battlefield.

B.E.S.T.

The Supreme Minister's husband Xander Forte ran a campaign insisting Europe needed one central person responsible for ensuring its safety. He amped up his countrymen's fear of Russia and the Middle East, claiming he would build an army to protect all native Europeans. When it came time for citizens to vote, he was the only one willing to take on the role, and was elected into the new position unchallenged.

Xander Forte's army suffered high turnover due to deadly attacks and those defecting to the rebel side. Caught off guard by a mob of hundreds, Xander and several dozen of his supposed protectors were gunned down outside the newly-formed Capitol building in Vienna. The pushy press and terrorized population of Europe thrust Jordynna Forte into her husband's role as Supreme Minister, never once asking if she wanted the same responsibility. She didn't.

She took the title forced upon her, but made no effort to revive her husband's efforts. Jordynna confided in Colonel Harrison that she had no interest in risking her life to become a hero when she was first invited to this summit. The Colonel tugged at her conscience and sense of duty, guilting her heart into overruling her head and showing up in spite of her fears.

"Government is ineffective, anyone remaining in law enforcement is a corrupt criminal, and everyday citizens have lost their sense of purpose. The poor are severely outnumbered by the grotesquely rich. They have nothing to lose and will overthrow anyone with money and power. The wealthiest one-percent was the first classification to go extinct at the hands of gang members and drug addicts chasing their next high. Why would anyone want to get involved in fixing this world, when they know anything valuable they obtain will be stolen later on?" The Supreme Minister posed her question directly to Colonel Harrison.

The current world wasn't exactly a world worth living in, let alone worth donating to its survival. Amica knew a safer, secure world would be worth buying into and that she had a plan to achieve exactly that. Her mind rapidly assessed, adjusted, and relaunched a better approach to the meeting within seconds of recognizing the roadblock. It was essential that she maintained their confidence if she was ever going to pull this plan off.

"Maybe we need to offer an incentive; give them something for their contribution that can't be taken away?" The Colonel had been fantasizing about her version of a utopia for months and knew it would only work if everyone contributed and benefited. She wondered how many other people would pay for the opportunity to live in a truly equal society, separate from those who intend to cause harm.

Amica continued, "Instead of viewing it as a donation, what if we propose it more like a market share or a spot in our new community. People can bid either money, supplies, or services to the various projects we need and that guarantees them a spot in the utopia we build."

"I thought we were just cleaning the oceans and creating better environmental policies?" Doctor Romano was standing in the hall with Ariel when the conversation in the next room caught her attention, "What exactly are we building?"

"There's more to my idea than just fixing the environmental damage; we need to rebuild an entire section of earth and make it a sustainable place to thrive for those who help create it. And we need to segregate our new utopia from the toxic areas surrounding it." Amica knew how bizarre her suggestion sounded. She had the entire plan tucked securely in the crevice of her mind, but wasn't ready to reveal the whole scope of her intentions.

"Where would this utopia be? How can we keep anybody out of this section of earth?" The Supreme Minister Forte quickly fired back. "Everyone has a right to walk freely about, and if you still owe a gun, you can force your way into anywhere. Anything we create will be overrun by rebels eventually."

"We're only nine women; even with our waning political influence, we can't fight to protect any significant mass of land. I am a Commander without an army," Commander Mei Ying tossed her concerns into their discussion.

"You keep alluding to some secret plan to keep us safe. I think you owe us more information if you expect us to continue working with you." Dr. Martin joined the rest of the ladies, who had now regathered in the main living space.

"Those exact feelings of doubt are the reason I haven't delved too deeply into everything on our agenda. I don't want us to have a need for an army or to use violence as a solution, which I understand sounds quite far-fetched." The Colonel held her hands up, palms facing the group. "If I want you to trust in me, then I need to show trust in you.

"I have a plan regarding how to make our new world secure, and regrettably it borrows a few ideas from the 2016 and 2020 American elections, including a border wall that we will make out of recyclables and a relocation plan for dangerous criminals." Amica ignored the widening eyes and continued explaining without revealing too many details.

"To improve our chances of success, we need to tackle the various tasks in stages. I promise to reveal a plausible defense strategy that doesn't require us physically fighting our enemies, however we can't get there without laborers and more resources. That's our main focus right now: people and supplies." The Colonel's tone was curt and authoritative, prompting silence.

Colonel Amica Harrison recognized that they had made a bit of progress, but there were too many frustrations just within the first few hours of forming her B.E.S.T. alliance. Not wanting tensions to heighten or a loss of enthusiasm, she wrapped up the day by celebrating what they did accomplish.

"Thank you so much for believing in this idea and putting in a valiant effort today in spite of the frustrations. I would like to go around the room and recap our progress." As she spoke, the Colonel's assistant Arturo changed the slide on the screen behind her to the four questions at hand.

"Let's start with Dawna. Who were you able to recruit?"

"My cousin Alexa, who's a homeschool teacher, my fifteen-year-old son Anderson, my neighbors Bella and Josée, who both have military experience, and two environmental engineers who have worked with the EPA, Oliver and Zoey," Dawna stated stiffly.

"That's a great start. We'll meet again next week at a bigger venue with the new recruits and divide everyone into groups based on their skill sets and passions. Thank you!" Amica gave her friend a big smile in return before proceeding with her questions. "How much money did you raise?"

"Only six hundred dollars from four different people, and I believe they only donated so I would stop making them feel guilty. A

Leamington farmer my father used to work with is sending us four barrels of baby cucumbers, ten jumbo jars of pickles, and a few pounds of garlic and dill." Dawna double-checked her tally sheet after reciting the totals from memory.

"Every cent helps, and food will be crucial as we recruit more people. What was your greatest success story from today?" The Colonel continued.

"The people who did agree to participate were thrilled to hear someone still cared enough about the world to try to save it," Dawna replied with a noticeable increase in enthusiasm.

"What was the greatest challenge?" Amica inquired with sincerity.

"Trying to convince people that hope was a good enough reason to invest their time and/or money." Dawna answered quite quickly.

"Yes, I expect that was a big struggle for everyone. I might have a solution to that one, but I'll go over my ideas at the end. Kali, can you answer the same four questions, starting with how many people you were able to recruit?" Colonel Harrison gestured a thank you to Dawna before turning to hear Kali's update.

Each woman shared the handful of names they recruited, the minimal money they collected, and similar successes and challenges. Arturo updated a detailed chart totalling the recruits, donations, successes, and challenges as each woman spoke.

"It was not an easy request that I made a few hours ago, yet we still managed to inspire forty-nine people to join us and collected almost seven thousand dollars in pledges. That's what nine women can do in less than three hours. Let's give ourselves a round of applause for inspiring hope at this critical moment in history." Colonel Harrison clapped her hands together loudly while the unimpressed crowd around her tossed in a half-hearted, light palm smack.

"Well, we tried, and it's nowhere near what we need to succeed. There are thousands of rebels in the South with millions of dollars who could wipe us out in the blink of an eye. Are we still doing this?" Doctor Martin's tone of dissension doused her rally cry with doubt.

"I knew this would not be an easy endeavor and today was only the beginning. That's why we started with this impressive team of creative, capable, and committed women. You have the education, experience, and tenacity to get the job done. You're also fierce advocates online and have impressive connections on social media that you can use to grow our community." The reference to social media slipped from her lips far earlier than she intended, a mistake her pragmatic mind rarely made.

As much as she couldn't go into specifics of the campaign at this time, the Colonel knew she had to give them enough information in order to revive their passion and motivate them to continue. It was a wild premise to base a plan on and she feared some may not see its brilliance. However, they needed reassurance, and she was all in now. A deep inhale, and she exhaled the idea, slowly and carefully.

"I think we can use your social media reach to our advantage. The reason no one cares about cleaning our oceans and fixing our ecosystem is because the world is in a state of constant war. Violent crimes are an epidemic that have become just as destructive as the catastrophic climate crisis. Both problems need to be solved simultaneously, or our efforts won't matter."

Every woman stared back into the Colonel's blue eyes while she stated once again the stark reality of their mission. They were drawn in by the passion burning within her as they clung to every word. "We need to recreate a society that shares a respect for human life and our core values of equality. We need a world free from greed and violence. My plan is to create a literal utopia, as fantastical or unrealistic as that sounds. We are building a world where everyone can be themselves without fear of persecution."

"That sounds like a lovely fantasy that has yet to exist throughout the history of mankind and most likely never will," Prime Minister Cortez quipped back.

"It's possible if it only contains like-minded people. What if we turned our political divide into a physical divide?" Colonel Harrison carried on with every ounce of confidence she could muster.

"It's too costly to travel from one continent to another for most people, but not for the criminals who robbed and slaughtered the wealthy. They are stockpiling in the South and plan to eradicate as many people as possible to prolong their own existence. We need to think the same way. I have a plan to get the worst people in this world to relocate to the same place as one another, far away from us. We will send them somewhere where they can kill themselves off, allowing the rest of us to live in peace."

Her voice gave the illusion of calm; her eyes focused on her teammates. Every face blankly stared back at her, looking perplexed and doubtful. The experienced Colonel summarized the general concept for the misinformation campaign, which would later be known as BEST's Map to Utopia, while the women listened with jaws steadily dropping wider. There were still many details to hash out and some holes in the execution strategy, yet it was enough to inspire the women to continue.

"Wow, that is actually plausible. It honestly could work," Prime Minister Cortez said quietly while nodding in agreement. "Now I'm excited to head back home and get ready for the swap in Australia. I'll make sure I'm only bringing the best people with me. Please let me know when you expect the riff raff to arrive."

"There's still a lot of work that needs to be done first, but preparing your country will be your primary focus for the next few months. Relocating the rebels will take place during the second phase of the plan, once we build our team and secure the border. Gather everything and everyone you trust in the meantime; I'll stay in touch as we progress. This crazy idea is our best course of action and we'll take it one careful step at a time," Colonel Harrison replied.

"I think it's time for us to call it a day. Today was more productive than you may think and we will connect again in a few days. Artuoro will send a meeting invite alert once I determine a day and place that works. I'll choose a location as close to here as possible and secure accommodations for those coming from far away. Thank you, ladies. We are the heroes this world needs!"

The women mingled briefly, thanking each other for their contributions and then separating for the night. The Colonel checked in with Royelle, who was still in the kitchen producing nutrient supplements for their future team members, before retreating to her office to finalize the details she had been sorting out for months. It was too early to tell, but her gut assured her that their tiny hope in hell would actually be enough.

Building An Army

The next few days flew by in a frantic blur. The Colonel and her best friend Royelle packed and hauled everything they could possibly need from their shared cabin in Smiths Falls, their individual townhouses in Hamilton, and Amica's office at EPC Global. Royelle owned a bakery/convenience store in Hamilton, which they enthusiastically emptied into her tiny Chevy Bolt and Amica's Company-issued Cargo POP.

POPs were Personal Operational Planes that came in three sizes, Cargo (two-seater, maximum weight two thousand pounds, Commuter two-seater, maximum weight twelve hundred pounds) and the Mini (one-seater, maximum weight seven hundred and fifty pounds). The big cargo-carrier model cost well over two hundred thousand dollars and far exceeded what the Colonel could afford to spend on such a luxury. Conveniently, before the gracious owner of EPC passed away from Cholera due to a contaminated water supply in Michigan, he would allow Amica to use the company's POP to transport equipment to the Great Lakes. The Colonel assumed she'd have his blessing to use the handy vehicle for her current efforts to save the planet, since it was parked at her cabin and no one else had laid claim to it.

It took two days and four trips to move everything they owned onto an old army base in Trenton, Ontario. Once they were fully unloaded and somewhat unpacked, Amica, Royelle, and Arturo went for a drive around the area in search of suitable housing for their new teammates.

Most Canadians who originally lived in that area chose to relocate to larger cities like Toronto and Ottawa once basic resources became scarce. There was an empty retirement residence, an old military resource center, rows of empty refugee housing, and a worn-down Ramada Inn all located within a few kilometers of the Army base. Layers of dust and debris covered nearly everything, but the potential for quality housing was everywhere.

"I know you have a million things to get done before everyone returns in a few days. I'll work with Arturo to get the rooms ready and create a meal plan while you work your magic on strategizing how to keep this snowball rolling," Royelle generously volunteered and grinned when she heard a sigh of relief escaped from her dear friend.

"Thank you, Royelle! I don't think I would have the guts to attempt any of this if I didn't have your support." Amica squeezed her friend with the utmost sincerity.

"You'll always have me on your team. I believe in you, even when you're borrowing pages from Putin's playbook and Trump's racist agenda," The blonde-haired, blue-eyed angel teased her lifelong friend.

"Ouch! Yeah, I'm shocking myself. We need every trick in the book to pull this off, and at least our wall has a dual, environmentally-friendly purpose. Sometimes the bad guys have good ideas, and the good guys have bad ideas. That's what would have fixed this shit decades ago: compromise and collaboration. Both sides needed to work together, meet in the middle, and save the planet before it got this bad. Now we're the last line of defense and it's time to get off our high horses and battle for the future of the world." Amica's voice rose with each word she rambled, her arms becoming animated and fists clenched in passion.

"Settle down, dude. I know, and I'm not judging, just teasing. I love your plan and can't wait to see it in action," Royelle quipped back.

"If you would have told me twenty years ago that I'd be advocating for a border wall, I would have laughed at you. Guess I've changed with the times," Amica reluctantly admitted.

"The times have changed us, and that's okay," Royelle assured her.

They wrapped their arms around one another in a meaningful, encompassing hug before separating for the remainder of the day. Amica's next task was to track down as many former military members as she could, including several pilots and at least one person capable of steering a massive freight liner, and then convince them that her plan would work. Finding them using social media was the easy part. Giving them a sense of hope after everything they saw working for the government was the real challenge.

Forty-nine new recruits arrived at Colonel Harrison's old base in Trenton, along with the twelve former-military women and men the Colonel asked to participate. Her assistant Aurturo, her best friend Royelle, and the nine leaders from the Smith Falls meeting brought

B.E.S.T.'s total to seventy-two people in less than ten days. The old worn-down mess hall had not been that full in over a decade.

"Thank you so much for coming here today. I know faith is a commodity in short supply these days and I appreciate your faith in myself and the others who asked you to partake in this massive endeavor. Our world is worth saving and we can honestly do it if we work together." A few quiet claps echoed in the room, but the majority were listening too intently to make a sound.

The Colonel went over the general plans, divided the attendees into the same three groups, and assigned each group a task-specific agenda. Kali Robbins's team's main responsibility would be recruitment, fundraising, and promoting the benefits of living in their new utopia.

Dawna Marchard's team consisted of technical specialists, engineers, and environmental experts. Their goal would be to finalize plans for the filtration system, develop a beneficial repurposing program, and pursue other environmental avenues that would extend the life of our planet, more specifically in the region around the Great Lakes.

Colonel Harrison's list was the most detailed, her goals intentionally being the most difficult to achieve. The first plan of action was to develop immediate rules for their new society that would be agreed on by the founding seventy-two members. She had to get the wall underway, pick a team for the misinformation campaign, and work with Rahel to ensure every member had enough food to survive. She could visualize everything that needed to be done; putting it into action was overwhelming.

Amica was an overachiever since birth, as her mother warned her early on that she had to be an asset on this earth if she expected to survive past the age of fifty. Amica was twenty-two when she first heard her mother's ominous encouragement. Her mother was forty-seven and terminally ill with cancer. The advice was repeated several times before her mom took her last breath, alone at age forty-nine in 2027. Her cancer battle peaked during the second global pandemic and Amica was not allowed in the hospital for chemo treatments during her mother's final few days on earth.

Her mother was here and then gone without warning or chance to share a proper goodbye. Amica's first reaction was a self-destructive spiral, but it was those foreboding words that kept her from going too far to return. Amica had to prove her value and earn her place on this planet. Now she had a team relying on her ideas to fix a world that was almost too far gone to save.

The Colonel asked the fourteen women and six men on her team to suggest laws of the land that would promote proven environmental policies and social equality, while guaranteeing health and prosperity for all those involved.

"We need to go back to the basics, live as our ancestors did, and create a just society free from violence. We can start with a firm rule that guns will be outlawed and violence of any kind will result in immediate expulsion from the new world we create." Colonel Harrison began her planned proposal with passion.

Tobin, a new recruit, was quick to point out the flaw with the Colonel's first rule. "How will we be able to remove those who don't comply if we don't have guns?"

"That's a valid question. I created a map of our new world, and once we have enough laborers to build it, there will be a tunnel on the south side that we can use to transfer any troublemakers to the outside." Amica quickly explained.

"Outside? Are we building walls like the one along the Mexican border? How big is this new world? There are still millions, probably billions of people on earth. How can we keep everyone out of the new country we're creating?" Tobin stood up to continue his rapid line of questioning.

"I understand that all of this sounds quite implausible and it will take years to rebuild a new world that's safe and sustainable. What other choice do we have? If we do nothing, our earth won't exist in ten years. I have ideas on how to keep us segregated from the criminals running wild Stateside. First, we need to establish rules and find recruits willing to follow them. I need you to trust that I have a plan. Can you offer a little faith in me until I can prove it will work?" Amica's eyes pleaded with the agitated man.

"Yeah, you're right. There is no other option. I've run out of ideas. What choice do I have, but to trust that someone can make a difference?" Tobin gave in.

"We can all make a difference, but we'll make a far greater one by working together," Amica added in a gentle tone.

"I'll try anything at this point." Tobin sat back down as fast as he rose.

"Thank you. Are there any rules you would like to bring forth?" The Colonel offered.

"Yes, everyone must work. No freeloaders allowed," Tobin shouted from his seat.

"I agree. We'll need everyone's involvement to make this work, including children over the age of sixteen. Does thirty hours of work seem reasonable? If we keep it lower than the historical standard, we can entice more recruits to join the effort," Amica asked.

"How can we pay people for their work? What have we collected so far in donations? There's no way we will ever have enough," Brianna, another new recruit shouted as soon as the Colonel's last word slipped from her lips.

"Are you referring to the monetary donations that we will collect, Brianna?" The Colonel questioned.

"Yes. We'll need to get paid, otherwise people will quit," The heavy-set woman in her mid-forties stated matter-of-factly.

"Money is pretty close to being meaningless right now and can be stolen in seconds. Our new utopia will offer something of real value: community, security, and a future. We're collecting donations to buy equipment and supplies from some of the few manufacturers left on this side of the world. Anyone willing to work will be rewarded with the opportunity to live in the twenty-second century. They will receive food, housing, and hope. This is a matter of life or death. Is there anything else you would rather do with your time left on earth?" The kindness in the Colonel's tone shifted to sternness as she spoke.

Brianna slowly nodded in agreement, so Colonel Amica Harrison continued, "We need to stop thinking in terms of how the world was run before world war broke out. Old ways failed us and we need to create a new way of doing things that suits our current needs. I would like to finalize the contract for new recruits to sign this week, so for now, let's focus on establishing realistic guidelines for our new society. Does anyone have any other rules that we should all follow?"

The energy in the room calmed down, as the new members began contemplating what rules would work best for the majority of the population. In less than an hour, Amica's team created a simple contract with nine standard rules that everyone should be willing to follow.

The B.E.S.T. Community Commitment
Draft 1: June twenty-third, 2041
1. Violence of any kind will result in immediate expulsion from B.E.S.T.
2. All guns and weaponry are outlawed in B.E.S.T.
3. Tobacco and all opioids are illegal and usage will result in expulsion.
4. Every person over the age of sixteen must grow at least one crop in bulk, one outdoor tree, and a minimum of three houseplants, using recycled, purified rainwater.
5. Every person between the ages of sixteen and nineteen must work ten hours per week.
6. Every person twenty years old or older must work thirty hours per week until age sixty.
7. Reuse, reduce and recycle must be practiced whenever possible. Fines will be issued for abuse of natural or limited resources.

8. All food and general supplies will be rationed and divided equally among all members

9. Every person is equal to everyone else and no person shall be discriminated against or given special treatment for any reason.

Arturo created an electronic file and sent it by email to everyone who had signed up so far. He would be responsible for staying on top of the database of members and ensuring everyone agreed to the terms set forth by the founding members. If any changes were made, Arturo would send a revision alert to each member with the option to accept or challenge the change. A few weeks later, the request by their forestation expert Robert to add pesticides to the list of illegal substances was sent out to every member and passed unanimously.

It was a fair and reasonable set of expectations and they already made plenty of progress, especially given that it was most people's first day. Amica knew better than to push anyone too far, so she encouraged them to take a fifteen minute social break while she went to discuss their progress with Kali Robbin's team.

"Hi, Kali. Our team has put together a contract for our B.E.S.T. community. Arturo will forward you a copy, so please let me know if you have any concerns when you see it," The Colonel advised her kind and creative colleague.

"Of course, Amica. Is there anything else you need?" Kali inquired.

"Yes, moving forward, we will need to send a copy of the community commitment to every new recruit you sign up. Please make sure to copy Arturo on the email trail. He'll keep track of everything. How are the recruitment efforts going?" Amica eyes widened with the hope that today had been more productive.

"Really good, actually! Having more people working the phones has definitely resulted in more recruits. We must have signed up at least fifty new people today and raised thousands." Kali was clearly giddy over their progress. "Kristie, can you come here for a moment?"

Kali called over to a petite redhead who couldn't be older than twenty. The young yet confident woman jumped from her chair and scurried over to the Colonel, greeting her with an official salute.

"Yes, Miss Robbins. How can I help you?" Kristie's eyes sparkled with enthusiasm.

"You've already helped so much. I wanted to share the good news with the Colonel. Please tell her about the community in Leamington that wants to get involved with us." Kali turned their attention towards the young volunteer.

"My family owns two large greenhouses and we have friends in the agricultural community. Their property is currently tended and guarded by laborers who work in exchange for crops. They are trying to rebuild their own mini world, but are completely on board with the idea of working with us. My parents are having a meeting at their farmhouse tonight to register as many recruits as possible. We have tomatoes, cucumbers, peppers, basil, cannabis, strawberries, apples, and huge pumpkins in the early fall." Her rosy face beamed brighter with each sentence.

"Wow! That is wonderful news. We need farmers more than anything, and Windsor-Essex County is a viable area we need a foothold in. I plan to extend the border to include all of the Great Lakes. Now we can set up a separate homebase and food service station at each end of our map. Thanks to you, Kristie! This will be a huge help." The Colonel was grinning over how well this was suddenly working out.

"You're welcome. I think most people want to help, they just don't believe they can make a difference." Kristie's big smile grew wider before adding, "I knew that I could make a difference, and I'm good at convincing people that they can do good things, too."

The Colonel had no words for the young lady who was wise beyond her years. She gave Kristie a lengthy, solid clap, followed by a slow nod of appreciation, as she lost her focus temporarily, pondering the forming of their new reality. Amica's vision for utopia was expanding rapidly in her head while she absorbed how far along they were already after such a short period of time. She expected it would take months, if not years, to gather enough people to even start rebuilding the world. Things were moving faster than she anticipated and she needed to revise her intended boundaries and timeline.

The Colonel thanked both ladies, checked in with Dawna to see if they needed anything, and then returned to her team. Her next plan of action was creating work groupings based on her list of tasks. The three distinct groups needed to be broken down into all of the various job assignments they would need to tackle.

"We're currently divided into three teams, focusing on Balance, Equity, and Stability. I came up with the acronym B.E.S.T. because that's simply what we are doing. We're trying our best to sustain a livable environment. The T stands for teamwork and will include all laborers and teenagers over the age of sixteen." Arturo updated the slideshow to show the Colonel's plans for dividing each team by the various tasks as Amica spoke.

"I created general categories based on the tasks I foresee us needing in the new world. I would love some input regarding what other roles will be required." The Colonel posed the question to the group who was eagerly scanning the chart for more clarity on her plan of action.

"I don't see doctors or nurses on the list." Tobin was the first to answer, once again.

"Excellent point. We already have a few doctors on our team and I plan on reaching out to Ontario General Hospital for their involvement. I have a friend there who I think will be able to gather additional support." Arturo updated the list with "Doctors and hospital staff."

"Why are social media influencers a job?" Amanada, one of the few women on the team who was over the age of fifty, shouted next.

"It will be an important part of keeping our world safe. For the time being, I need to limit those who know the full scope of the project for security purposes," Amica explained.

"If we're all an equal member in this project, shouldn't we have the rights to the same information? TikTok and Twitter can't defend us against guns and bombs," Jodi snapped back.

"Jodi, are you old enough to remember the 2016 American election?" The Colonel herself was just starting high school when the Russians used bots and fake news articles to manipulate Americans into voting for Donald Trump Senior after a filthy audio recording of him was released just before the election. Outrageous yet convincing lies of his opponent flooded social media, and no one knew who to believe.

Using only social media, Putin and other adversaries turned politician partisanship into a massive divide between the Democrats and Republicans. Each side felt certain the other side was the responsible party and the conspiracies only amplified. Putin disappeared to die in secret long before he could see the true destruction of his handiwork.

"Yes, I do." Her eyes widened, and her tense lips lifted into a smile. "My interest has been piqued. Not sure how you can pull that off, but I have a social media background and can help spread any message you need. When I was putting myself through school in 2018, I made money as a beauty blogger. I still have a significant following."

"Wonderful! We will discuss how you can benefit the campaign when it's time to launch it. I want everyone to freely choose a role that suits them best. I'll put together the social media strategists team, but other than that, every position is available. If there's an imbalance or a position that no one wants to do, we can come up with a worthwhile incentive to inspire volunteers," Colonel Harrison explained further.

"How will we decide on the incentive? Doctors should obviously have more of an incentive to work than laborers or influencers. There has to be a pay system." Tobin jumped up again.

"Doctors need people to grow and prepare food, otherwise they wouldn't survive," Josée responded eagerly and enthusiastically, before turning towards, "Didn't mean to interject, but if it's going to be a truly equal society, we're all equally valuable.

"Josée is right. Every contribution is just as necessary as the rest. We won't have a secure country without building a solid permeter out of non-recyclables. We need people to tend to the forests and lakes, just as much we will need medical professionals. Incentives will only be offered for the tasks that no one is willing to do. I'm sure those things will happen, as I'm personally not willing to work in a morgue or a sanitation plant." The Colonel joked a bit to lighten the growing tension. Sadly, she was unsuccessful.

"Now this is sounding like a socialist dictatorship. I'm not giving up my right to make good money," A lanky younger man said loudly to the woman next to him.

"We need to elect a proper government," Another voice from the crowd exclaimed.

"I don't trust governments. Everyone is supposed to have a say in what happens," Jodi interjected.

"This will never work," Amica heard someone else mumble.

The Colonel raised her arms high into the air, pulsating them back and forth slightly to attract their attention. "Please give this a chance and hear me out," She called into the crowd. "I need you to have faith in my intentions and trust that there is a strategic plan unfolding."

"I've only provided everyone here with an outline of what I think can save this world; I'm open to suggestions. I have thought out plans to back up each of my ideas, however, you can dispute anything you disagree with and it will be decided by a majority. If you don't agree with something we're doing as a society, there will be a grievance process and we'll put the matter to a vote.

"The three founding members, myself, Kali Robbins, and Dawna Marchand, will only get involved if the vote is within two percent. That way everyone is involved in the process. Does that help ease your concerns?" The Colonel paused and waited for heads to bob in agreement.

The group settled down and the aggressive questioning halted. After a few minutes of asking probing questions, the Colonel felt it was time to wrap up their discussion before any remaining enthusiasm had been swept away in distrust. She chose to celebrate it as a productive day with promise. Pushing new members would only scare them away.

"I want to reassure this group that we are all like-minded. I have a source in Canadian intelligence and a lifelong friend at Google helping our efforts from afar. They will be joining us once we officially exist. I used those contacts to vet every person in this building. They both confirmed that you are all peace-loving, anti-violence, accepting, kind, highly-skilled individuals. We want the same thing, a healthy planet and promising future, and we can achieve it by having faith in each other!" Colonel Harrison cheered into her team members' concerned faces.

"Today was productive and tomorrow will be even better. We've now been able to secure dozens of used tires and plastic frames for raw material, as well as two flatbeds for transporting the wall, thanks to Calvin and John on Dawna's team. One of our new members, Kristie, has connections with several large functional farms, which we'll obviously need to survive.

"Please head back to the room we've supplied for you on base, reach out to family and friends you trust, and grow this initiative. If you know of anyone running a reputable business in Ontario, Michigan, New York, Connecticut, etc., please ask for their support. Remember, not everyone needs to move here to be a part of the B.E.S.T. movement.

"We can cover what's left of Canada, starting with Ontario and Quebec. I don't want to go too far South, but we need to at least surround the Great Lakes with enough land on the other side to build a fourteen-foot-high by six-feet-wide wall. I want to leave hundreds of miles between us and the Southerners."

"Did you say six feet wide? Why so wide? Do you realize how thick that is?" Tobin interjected, yet again.

"Arturo, can you please show everyone the wall blueprints?" He changed the presentation to her clever design even before she could finish asking for it. "As you can see, the wall is a web of sharp, tall poles being held in place by old rubber tires and quick-set cement. We've developed an easy way to melt plastic into this slippery glass-like substance that is too slick to scale. I have samples of the finished pieces that I can bring with me tomorrow."

"If we make it with a three-inch diameter, it will be too thick to cut with a snip, but not wide enough that you could balance on top of it. They will be staggered close enough together at the bottom that you can't squeeze through them, with every other pole only being nine feet high, so they're not so close at the top that you can stand on two at once," Amica explained while pointing to parts of the diagram.

"Why fourteen feet high? Is that not a bit excessive?" Antonio, the contractor who Amica emailed with structural questions during the design, pondered out loud. "I didn't think of it when we discussed it prior, but you can save precious material by capping the wall at twelve feet. The poles will still be too slippery for anyone to climb."

"Each component will be approximately seventeen feet high, with the first two tires buried underground. POPs can fly up to twelve feet high, which is why the finished height should be closer to fourteen. I don't want to risk being attacked by personal planes," Colonel Harrison responded without hesitation. She had a reason for each measurement, but didn't feel the need to explain herself in nauseating detail. Without direction, her best friend instinctually leapt to her defense.

"The Colonel has fussed over the design for months to ensure it will keep intruders out. There is a reason for every specification that has been reviewed by Dawna, Kali, Arturo, and myself. She also shared it with Antonio, who is a general contractor and engineer. He confirmed it would serve us well," Royelle assured the group with genuine sincerity.

Amica gave her dear companion a quick nod of appreciation before continuing her send-off for the evening. "These are brainstorming sessions; no decision is final if the majority feels we need to make changes. Once we know exactly who wants to be a part of this new world, we will vote on a specific border before we construct any portion of the wall.

"Take some time tonight and think over my proposed design. If there's a flaw in my idea, please let me know. Get some rest and show up tomorrow morning whenever you're ready. We'll brainstorm what needs to be done and assign priority rankings to each task. The other groups are building an army of supporters and the equipment to make this happen. It's our job to create a solid plan of action to put their efforts to good use."

After her team left, Amica printed a copy of the roles assigned to each team for Kali and Dawna. Both looked exhausted upon approach, so she encouraged them to wrap up their group for the day as well.

"I appreciate all of your help and this can certainly wait until tomorrow, but I would like you to present these roles to your team members for their feedback. Please let me know if there are any concerns or changes. How was the energy in your group today?"

"Mostly good. A few had a hard time recruiting resources or raising funds, but are willing to help others stay organized," Kali answered first.

"I haven't had this much fun collaborating with a team since we first started working together... Of course that was before the world began self-imploding. There's actually hope again that something can be done. I needed to feel that and am ready to tackle the Great Lakes!" Dawna vocalized the enthusiasm her exhaustion was hiding.

"Me too," Amica whispered.

"Me too," Kali stated.

Colonel Harrison smiled and retreated without saying another word. Inspiring hope gave her mixed feelings. She had all these ideas that made sense when she plotted them out on her tablet. Anything can sound like a good plan in theory, the only thing that truly matters is what it's like once it's in action.

After the sessions were over and everyone dispersed for the day, Colonel Harrison retired to her office. There was still so much more work to do. She finally felt confident enough to share her plans with former business contacts and some of the companies that were still attempting to conduct business as normal without an official government keeping them in check.

After the assassination of the third Prime Minister in a row, politicians started resigning at rapid speed. Prime Minister Kait Schwartz was the first female Prime Minister elected by the people in 2039. The majority of Canadians, including Kait, naively assumed that no one would try to kill a woman. She ran on a platform of peace and equality for all Canadians and had sound plans regarding how to reverse the damage caused by the climate crisis. Six months later, Kait and her wife were shot by a sniper while exchanging a quick kiss outside of a bookstore.

Her predecessor, Prime Minister Elliot Francois, was a cost-cutting conservative who was killed by an angry protester after he cut government-funded mental health care coverage. The previous Prime Minister to Schwartz was another idealistic liberal that was also shot by a sniper that had never been captured. Six other members of Parliament, two mayors, dozens of city officials, and the Head of the Toronto police all lost their lives to angry Canadians between 2034 and 2040. The chaos from the former United States of America had trickled into Canada and no one felt safe.

B.E.S.T.

Most traditional news stations and media companies collapsed with the government, but there were a few still trying to stay afloat. Bell Media, Global, and Cogeco provided scattered broadcasts, mostly online. The Colonel was interviewed by a correspondent at Bell Media when the Canadian military pulled their troops out of the conflict in the United States. She also had a cousin who worked in advertising sales at the Global Television Network. She would need their resources for her disinformation campaign and as a communication tool for their new world.

Good Morning Reputable Journalists,

I'm sending this message in hopes that we share similar beliefs and can team up to repair the earth and reduce rebel violence. I have not lost hope and fortunately I am no longer alone in my belief that our world can be saved. We are already working on building a solid foundation for a better future. If you feel the same way, please respond to signify your support.

My non-violent plan to remove anyone who values guns and money more than human life will only be successful if I have your full cooperation. I need two contradictory stories spread globally without question.

If I receive confirmation that you're willing to go along with this plan without needing any further details, I'll follow up with the articles when it's time to go public with them. Until then, I beg that you do not disclose receipt of this email to anyone. One hundred percent confidentiality is critical to the success of our efforts to save this planet.

Stay safe, sincerely,

Colonel Amica J. Harrison

The Colonel slowly read each word out loud while scanning the email for proper spelling and punctuation. The email had been parked in her draft folder for weeks and it was the umpteenth time she gave each pending word a careful reconsideration. She scanned the list of twenty-nine names that were blindly carbon-copied, mentally checking each one for any chance her message could backfire. Amica had already done thorough background and social media checks on each one of these potential allies. She knew everyone copied was a fighter for equality and environmental reform, or at least appeared to be so on social media.

"Nothing to fear except fear itself," she whispered to the empty room.

Today proved there was enough support to put her plan into action; she could not delay it any longer. Amica's stomach rumbled in protest and her breathing slowed to a stop as her clammy index finger tapped the enter key. Done. She sent a quick prayer to the heavens that the response would be positive before retiring to her new bedroom.

Amica tossed and turned all night, wondering if she should feel as skeptical as the new recruits looked. She knew the holes in her plan were larger than most of the sinkholes currently swallowing up New York's former financial district. What if she couldn't trick the criminals into relocating? What if the area she chose to rebuild the world on actually sank into the Great Lakes? The possibility of her plan falling apart was as real as the threat of total extinction if they sat back and did nothing. Did she really want the burden of failure on her shoulders?

Amica finally gave up on sleep shortly after five am. The Colonel preferred to savor several cups of daffodil tea alone before anyone else woke up. She also wanted to squeeze in a little exercise first. She went for a slow jog around the old army base as the brilliant sun rose around her. Heaps of trash, burned-out buildings, and rotting animal flesh could be seen in every direction. Amica kept her head towards the sky as it changed from gray to blue.

The twisted honeysuckle tree at the end of her new morning route broke through the devastating scene with its mighty resilience. It towered over the wreckage, thick arms spreading into the clouds. The tall tree's rough bark clung to its three-pronged trunk, brittle with age. Snapped auburn branches were suspended amongst the vibrant green dangling pods.

"It must be older than I am," Amica thought out loud to herself. *"And yet, it is still standing."*

The reality of the broken earth surrounded by a massive tree that stood the test of time only fueled Amica to push her body faster. It was exceptionally warm weather and her handmade headband couldn't stop the salty sweat from dripping into her eyes. She stumbled back to base, physically drained and mentally determined.

B.E.S.T.

The Colonel stopped dead in her tracks when she rounded the last corner. She had not seen anyone along her route and now there was a sizable crowd. Kali, Dawna, Prime Minister Cortez, Doctor Martin, Royelle, Arturo, Josée, Tobin, Jodi, and at least two dozen other faces she didn't recognize were waiting at the doorstep to her new residence.

"What's wrong?" She shouted towards the unexpected group spread out in front of her.

"Nothing is wrong, Colonel. We're just eager to make this supposed utopia our reality," Dawna answered with a massive grin on her face.

The sweat in Amica's eyes transformed into tears. She took a moment to soak in the energy bursting from the happy souls in front of her before waving her arms in the direction of the group training center. Without giving a verbal command, everyone followed the Colonel inside the building.

Her emotions were running amok as she fought off flashbacks of everything it took to get to this point. Amica wasn't always a respected Colonel. Though her life was guided into the life of a prodigy right from the beginning, it took a dramatic, rebellious turn before she signed up for the Canadian military.

After graduating high school, Amica chose to follow a less traditional path. She picked up a waitressing job at a local nightclub and sold safer cosmetics online for a multi-level marketing company. She made just enough money to blow it all on booze and expensive clothing while struggling to afford her rent and utilities. The consensus amongst her peers was the world only had a few years left, so they might as well enjoy their limited time on earth.

Some days she enjoyed it a little too much.

Some nights she regrets, some nights she can't remember at all.

Amica Harrison joined the military at age twenty-three, after she scared herself by choosing to drive after drinking far too much alcohol. The world wasn't ending as fast as she thought it would, and if she wasn't careful, she would be the one responsible for her death instead of climate change or the next world war. She couldn't waste her life if there would still be life left to live. Amica was tempted to turn towards alcohol again when her mother died the following year, but it was the self-discipline she was learning in the army that stopped her from losing herself in the bottle.

There were many days when Amica felt like she would never make a difference, and now she was leading an army in an effort to save the world. All of her training, planning, and researching had prepared her for this unbelievable challenge. It felt so surreal in the moment that it allowed Amica to disassociate herself long enough not to get swept away by her emotions.

A quick inner shake off, and The Colonel approached the front podium with calm and confidence. She started by clapping enthusiastically and she made eye contact with each person in front of her.

"Thank you! Look around at your fellow human beings and say thank you. Everyone is here today because they know the planet is worth saving and we can only save it by working together. Thank you for caring enough to help. Thank you for having faith in me and my ideas!" Colonel Harrison cheered into the crowd and they roared back loudly in support.

"We're ready. There are enough of us now to start unrolling our plans. Dawna's team is ready to start filtering the Great Lakes free from debris and we have enough material and team members to begin building our border. We'll keep growing and continue to have members fundraising and recruiting while we create physical progress.

"If there is anyone on my team or Kali's that wants to be a part of either the lake filtration team, forest clean-up, or building our wall of non-recyclable materials, please let Arturo know before joining your new group. I want to track where everyone is working for safety and security reasons.

"Dawna will be the captain of the lake clean-up team; Robert, Algonquin Park's forest ranger, will organize the forest clean-up and replanting. Doctor Sinclair and Calvin will train the team constructing the plastic pipes and tires for the border. Royelle and Kristie will also be working together to sort and prepare food supplies for everyone. I'm sure they could use help as well, considering how many mouths we now have to feed.

"Once we begin building the wall, those who stay back can either help in the kitchen or work with Kali Robbins on generating more recruits and supplies. After the border is underway, I'll need a team to help me prioritize the next steps we need to take. I want everyone to choose the work they do based on their skills and passions, so every member feels included and valued." Applauds echoed through the space as she paused to catch her breath.

As the roar faded, the Colonel continued her rally cry: "We can do this. We will do this! The people in front of me and the team surrounding us will save the world. We will! I believe in us."

Hooting and hollering filled the once orderly militant army base. She shouted back into the crowd, "Now, let's get to work," and everyone quickly broke into eager teams. The Colonel's group remained inside the training room.

"Good morning, team! Thank you for sticking with me. There are quite a few decisions we need to make today, including the most important one, finalizing our new world's boundaries. The southern border is obviously the most crucial, and is our first physical task." Arturo displayed an old map of the United States, prior to their second civil war, on the projection screen.

"Most of the rebels are scattered throughout Texas, Oklahoma, Arkansas, Tennessee, Mississippi,and Alabama. Based on my intel, the west coast is unlivable and most of the east coast is underwater. I feel we should focus on Manitoba, Ontario, and Quebec, as well as North and South Dakota, Minnesota, Illinois, Michigan, and New York. Any objections or concerns with those specifics?"

Not a sound rose from the thirty individuals in front of her, so she continued outlining the details she finalized last night: "The border separating Michigan from Ohio and Indiana should be our first focus, as southern anarchists are moving towards the old Kentucky area. I've secured the use of three solar-powered flatbeds and two Diesel freight trucks to transport the poles to the erection sites."

The Colonel paused for a moment, wondering how long it would take to build enough poles to fill the trucks and be ready for their first section. The walls' time frame varied based on the number of participants and how quickly they could obtain enough material. The Colonel would have to estimate and adjust if needed.

"Arturo, how many people are on Dr. Sinclair and Calvin's team right now?" Colonel Harrison asked mid-speech.

"Only seven, Colonel." One click of his wrist and Arturo quickly replied.

"That won't be enough people to fabricate the poles, and we will need significantly more when it comes time to construct it. After we're done planning here, I encourage anyone in this group who is willing to help with the wall production to move onto that team temporarily.

"We need to bury the base of the pole at least a foot deep, and I'm still trying to find us a big enough backhoe. I meant to ask Kristie earlier; the farmers she knows must use something powerful to dig. That brings me to our next focus: finalizing a list of jobs and priorities. New people keep showing up and it's essential we utilize everyone to the best of their abilities.

"We've secured truckloads of recycled building material, some of which are *en route* already. If we have any new recruits with truck-driving experience or a large vehicle, Arturo can assign them a truck and a partner to help with loading on site. Any engineers, electricians, or environmental specialists will be offered the chance to work on the water filtration advancement team. We have a smaller working model that Dawna will begin running through Lake Ontario. It will take months to cover every inch, so she'll need help to scale it large enough to cover twice the distance at double the speed.

"It's a big agenda, and a necessary one. Our world is teetering on the brink. We need to rebalance it, create true equality, and stabilize it for future generations. We can do that with teamwork, if we all try our best. I believe in us!" The Colonel repeated her previous cheer and her team erupted in loud clapping.

Unlike the day before, no one interrupted or questioned her plans. Tobin's only comment was that he knew several good men and women with forklift licenses who might be interested in getting involved. Amica graciously thanked him for looking into those specific recruitments. Doubt was gone, and together they plotted every immediate priority and plan of action.

Population Problems

Hundreds of volunteers turned into thousands within a matter of days, and everyone was eager to work. Arturo ended up requiring his own assistant, Ashley, just to keep track of the members and where each of them were working. There was a noticeable buzz of energy around the base and Amica had to act fast to capitalize on their enthusiasm.

Twenty-six food enthusiasts volunteered to work with Royelle and Kristie, preparing food and nutrient-boosters in the kitchen and garden. They already collected a wide range of vegetables and fruit from the new members to make vitamins for the crew.

In 2036, when food scarcity was causing even those with money to die from starvation, a company called Compost Harvest created a fermentation process to extract the nutrients from fruit rinds and vegetable peels. Inedible yet nutrient-enriched plants were added to the mix. They dehydrated the scraps after fermentation and converted them into pill form.

When Compost Harvest released their product it was only twenty dollars for two hundred pills, made mostly from corn husks, orange and carrot peels, and onion skins. It kept the scurvy away and was more affordable than anything else you could buy, so sales skyrocketed. The owner got a little greedy, and the price quickly became twenty dollars for fifty pills, more than anyone could actually afford.

Their success was short-lived when a TikTok influencer figured out how they were made and shared the secret with the world. Royelle and Kristie cut off the best pieces for stews, soups, and salads, extracted every seed for planting, and any piece that was not yummy enough to eat was tossed in a warm sea salt and vinegar bath. Nothing would, or should, be wasted.

Every member of B.E.S.T. was assigned a task that would benefit the entire team. Sixteen truck drivers were sent on errands to pick up various supplies, eleven eager members joined Robert in the forest, and nineteen skilled laborers wanted to work with Dawna on improving the efficiency of the water filtration system.

It didn't take long before they had a field stacked nearly ten feet high with thousands of bald, worn out tires and nine tons of recycled plastic that was waiting to be converted into sections for their new perimeter. Colonel Harrison convinced thousands of their new recruits to become part of the wall-building crew and everything started coming together faster than she ever imagined.

The beautifully diverse group of people from all walks of life worked as a human chain to roll the tires and barrels full of plastic into the fabrication facility. The plastic scrap pieces went in one direction to be melted down before formation, while the tires were handed over to a three-person production line on the right side of the entrance.

The first person drilled five pole holes using a punch press and then stacked the tires in groups of four. The second person separated the tires from each other by sticking fat metal spikes in between and then put one of the formed poles inside each of the five drilled holes, connecting the four tires together. The third person added four shorter poles in the center before pouring a fast-drying liquid cement mix to fill in any gaps in the holes, as well as the inside of the tire. The cement provided added durability and weight. Random able bodies floated throughout the process, helping to move the product from one person to the next.

Outside the door on the opposite end, there was a separate double line-up of people working together to carry the much heavier finished product back to open spaces in the field where the used tires had previously been removed. It was a magnificent cycle of non-recyclables being recycled and repurposed. The harmonious teamwork pumped out months' worth of work within the first ten days.

The budding team produced seven hundred two-foot by seventeen-foot structural pieces that filled the back end of the abandoned army base. Each one consisted of four stacked rubber tires (separated in the middle with steel spikes, creating a three inch gap) and five fourteen-foot-tall slippery hard plastic poles that were secured inside the stack of tires using more cement. There were also four more nine-foot-high poles in the center of the tires.

They 'borrowed' a crane from an abandoned construction company in Markham to load and unload the flatbeds and truck trailers that had been collected from various business connections and local truck drivers. They were also able to secure a backhoe, a forklift, several wheelbarrows, and two scoops to assist with the digging that they would pick up along their way to the Windsor/Detroit border.

B.E.S.T.

The B.E.S.T. community was roaring!

There was no room left on the base to move about; people, random vehicles, and transport trucks stacked with pieces of future wall filled every inch of the once-wide open fields. Everyone was eagerly waiting for the Colonel to outline their next step.

The Colonel stood frozen, surveying her massive team. Her lip trembled, fighting back tears of pride and rising fear. Amica was bursting with anticipation until the sight of their massive convoy awoke memories of the Colonel's first battle in the Canadian Army Forces. She was twenty-six years old, had excelled in her training, and was physically prepared for battle, or so she thought.

Amica was one of only thirteen women sent to the front lines of the Canadian border, and her imagination ran wild while they were *en route*. She heard stories of Americans forming chains along borders with automatic rifles, firing fast at anyone who came into their sight. Her heavy boots held her shaky legs in place while she sat motionless in the carrier for the nine-hour drive.

When their convoy stopped, Amica didn't want to get out. Her starched khakis felt as if they were stuck to the seat and her commander had to pull her by the arm into a standing position. One foot at a time, she stepped outside, found her spot alongside her team, and instantly transformed into the confident soldier she was trained to be. The Colonel had conquered her fear in that terrifying moment, and she knew she could again.

Her only hesitance came from how people on both sides of their new border would react once their plans were no longer a secret. There were still close to a million people spread out across Canada, and millions scattered in the Northern United States, choosing to lay low until the earth came to its ultimate demise. Amica paced while pondering the yet-to-be-answered questions that had been giving her random silver hairs since the idea first entered her mind.

How would they react to a giant wall dividing the continent in half?

How long before she'd have to pull the trigger on their most dangerous defense plan?

Would her plan even keep them safe?

Daily news alerts confirmed there was a real threat of associates from the New United Republic rebels terrorizing and killing northerners to expand their territory. As tropical storms tore deeper into the coast, southerners began moving north. Kentucky was being ravaged for resources and Indiana would soon follow.

If they saw the wall before it was physically long enough to keep everyone safe, it could quickly prove to be useless. The southerners had guns and weren't afraid to use them to take whatever they wanted. The further south they built, the more likely they would stumble on dangerous rebels prior to its completion.

It was time to take that massive leap, starting with the border tunnel. In the event that they encountered dangerous people on the northern side of the border, there would need to be a safe way to move them out. The Windsor-Detroit tunnel was an ideal choice, and was the only way across the Detroit River without a boat since the Ambassador bridge was destroyed by a suicide bomber in 2034. Their plans to rebuild the bridge never came to fruition due to the region's economic decline.

Amica gave her head a shake, pushing all the negative possibilities from her mind. They were ready to move to the next phase in her plan. Colonel Harrison addressed the team one last time, outlining the next steps they would be taking.

"It's time for us to build a wall. I know this is a sentence that's hard for most progressives to get behind. If we want a world without weapons, we must have some form of protection. We are replanting, cleaning, and restoring our ecosystem; those efforts can not be wasted. We can not let the threat of war destroy our hard work. This barrier will keep war from spoiling our efforts.

"Construction will begin where you exit the tunnel into Detroit and then move straight through most of Detroit, before starting to veer southwest. We need to surround Lake Michigan along the Indiana border and encompass all of Chicago. At the same time, we should build along the New York/Pennsylvania border to secure Lake Erie and the entire province of Ontario. If anyone gets lost along the way, our meeting point will be the Windsor entrance to the tunnel. It's right by their former casino.

"Royelle, Kristie, Arturo, Ariel, and myself will load the two weeks' worth of food and supplies we've prepared first thing tomorrow. Please get a good night's sleep because we will be leaving at seven am.

That will allow us enough time to stop at any communities along the way to drum up support and supplies."

The enthusiastic tone that her speech began with turned somber as she warned the untrained troops to expect the unexpected. "I haven't been south of the border since the war ended and can't predict what we might encounter tomorrow. Stay alert, stick together, and always remember your safety is your first priority. If you're willing to help with construction labor, please sign up with Arturo before retiring for the evening. I think we're ready. Who's with me?"

The last word hadn't yet left her lips when a flood of people swarmed Arturo, cheering loudly. Amica had to request more volunteers with meal prep because there were now two hundred and seven individuals volunteering for the build, plus another three dozen people who would work on gathering materials and converting the non-recyclables into more barriers back at the base.

Amica, Royelle, Kristie, Arturo, Supreme Minister Forte, and Doctor Sinclair helped put together three hundred and twenty nutrient-enriched snack bags containing two weeks of organic vitamin supplements, an apple, a pear, one large piece of chicken jerky, one hard-boiled egg, a tube of squeezable hummus, ten whole-grain bread chips, a small leaf salad with cucumbers, peppers, and onions, and one of Royelle's peanut, date, and honey protein bars.

Their supplies were quite limited, but fortunately they made arrangements with Kristie's farmer friends to pick up a few baskets of tomatoes, peppers, and cucumbers when they passed through on their way to the tunnel.

During their prep, Supreme Minister Forte snuck off for a few minutes to make a phone call before returning with a grateful grin. "I secured more recruits and more food!" The tiny woman pumped her fist high in the air in celebration. "My family and friends are gathering every canned good and scrap of food that's left in the European Union before boarding a naval ship for the east coast."

"Wonderful!" The Colonel shouted. "We're going to need it!"

"You'll also need someone to stay back and procure more meals for the team. We have small gardens blooming, there's fruit we can pick, and more seeds that need to be planted. I think we will need more food for our members before the end of the week," Royelle interjected.

"You're right! We also need an expert chef that can turn these fruits and vegetables into soups, sauces, and meals with substance. Are you offering your expertise?" Amica asked, knowing full well that was exactly what Royelle would want to be doing.

"Consider it done." Royelle winked with her consistently warm grin.

Royelle, Kristie, and Prime Minister Forte stayed back to help prepare more food for upcoming weeks on the road. Dawna, Ariel, Calvin, and a few dozen others stayed back to continue barrier-building production and lake filtration.

Colonel Harrison trusted the competent crew would keep things running smoothly in her absence. She was completely comfortable handing over the reins to other strong leaders, something her first commander in the Armed Forces used to say was the very reason she had never been promoted, 'If you let the other cadets think they have power, you'll lose yours.'

Amica's approach was different, and it wasn't until she met a female colonel named Tatyana Jackson that she encountered anyone in the army who validated her strategy. Colonel Jackson let Amica call her 'Tatyana' off duty and would remind her that they were equals in the grand scheme of life.

"Rank matters on the battlefield when life and death decisions are being made, but right here, right now, we are simply human beings. We're equals, trying to do our best for ourselves and those we love. In war, those who report to you must respect your authority and expertise while never forgetting that we're the same on the inside." Colonel Tatyana Jackson's wisdom was still guiding Colonel Amica Harrison through life.

Tatyana would approve of how Amica's cadets worked diligently alongside of her or just as hard when she was out of sight. They were equally invested in the success of the mission. The B.E.S.T. community members were in the process of building a new, sustainable world. The Colonel knew that willing participation and empowerment were essential to pull it off.

The wall erection team left the Trenton base a little later than expected and only made one stop in Leamington to meet the farmers and pick up extra vegetables for the crew. The major highway to

B.E.S.T.

Windsor was practically void of traffic and the few cars that did whizz by didn't slow anyone down. They proceeded through the unguarded Detroit tunnel into the broken country once known as the United States of America by mid-afternoon.

Wall construction was mapped out to begin at the Detroit River on Steve Yzerman Drive about one mile left of the tunnel. The pothole laden road curves south into I75, and the wall would follow alongside it to contain as much of Michigan as possible. From there they would build around Chicago, then head north to Wisconsin and Minnesota before re-entering Canada somewhere within Winnipeg.

Prior to departure, Colonel Harrison assigned each of the sixty-three vehicles in the convoy their own starting points. Heavy-duty equipment, trailers, flatbeds, and vans of supplies were spread out over the first eight miles of the border wall. Every vehicle had at least five team members so they could start unloading sections of the wall while they waited for a forklift to start digging the seven-foot-wide trenches.The tower of tires and poles would lay two tires deep, three by three, in a honeycomb fashion. The Colonel planned the process for maximum precision and marveled at how each step fell flawlessly into place.

Amica traveled inside the cab of the first flatbed. She helped carry massive structures to the site, shoveled the self-mixing gravel and cement mixture on top of the bottom two tires, which would solidify permanently the next time it rained, and then handed out meal packets to the volunteers once it was time to take a break. She asked Antonio to be the contractor responsible for the dig portion of the project, and Sarah, an experienced architect, was put in charge of where each piece would go. The Colonel's main focus was safety and morale.

The team members with military experience naturally kept an eye out for the rest, patrolling their surroundings whenever they were given a break from unloading and burying. Josée ran ahead of the group, searching nearby buildings for occupants or potential threats. A few others joined in, operating simultaneously in sync without ever verbalizing a command.

After the first five miles of the wall was erected, the lead group stopped to eat some of their prepared snacks. Josée made a beeline for the Colonel as soon as she saw her take a seat on the steps of a rundown movie theater. She was eager to offer insights into the many ways she could be more useful in their mission.

"Colonel Harrison, I have a few ideas, if you have some time to discuss?" Josée asked, hovering over Amica's shoulder from the step above her. The Colonel nodded, prompting her new friend to continue.

"I'm a Navy Seal with experience in the unimaginable. I broke free from the corrupt military so I could use my skills for vigilante justice rather than war for profitable misogynistic bullshit. If you need anything delicate or challenging resolved, I'm ready and willing." Her tiny yet rock-solid frame popped up straight up with an enthusiastic grin and respectful salute.

"Thank you, Josée. I'm sure something will arise that's suited to your skills. In fact, I could use your help right now. I was about to check a bunch of the buildings here, to see if we can find a place big enough for everyone to crash for the night. We will keep moving South, but when we rest, I want us to retreat, so we're at least partially protected."

"You got it! Let's go!" Josée's energy was electric and it set a fire under both women's feet as they began racing through the desolate streetways of River Rouge.

The two women took turns running in and out of buildings, providing each other with cover as they ran from floor to floor. The Colonel looked for any indication that someone had been there or possibly was still there, hiding, waiting to strike. They found a large, run-down museum that was next to a lot filled with tiny old school houses. It had enough space to securely fit the entire group inside.

The Colonel sent the empty trucks back to the base to reload for the next day, while the construction crew continued setting up the wall. The team erected approximately sixteen miles on the very first day, far exceeding the ten miles Amica had hoped they would manage.

When the sun faded from sight, the B.E.S.T. team slept alongside one another, spread out over a filthy carpet that smelled of wet dog and despair. It wasn't the first time Amica had to bunker down in filth; the smell wasn't what kept her tossing and turning. Her calcium-deficient bones ached from digging and lifting over and over again. Eventually, she crashed and slept soundlessly until the sun rose again.

Before heading out for the day, the Colonel selected a dozen troops from the team to guard the new territory they had claimed. The five women and seven men were instructed to use the museum as their home base. They were tasked with gathering everything they could from abandoned places surrounding them, and to hold tight. Colonel Harrison assured them she would return with more people and supplies in three days.

Day two brought them farther than the first day and they now had over forty miles of a border wall stretching south along Lake Erie. The second night, they chose an old hotel in Monroe, Michigan that appeared to be abandoned. Their feet and backs ached as they cautiously spread out, filling every room in the eighty-four-unit building within a matter of minutes.

The crew crashed anywhere they could that was remotely comfortable, while the Colonel gave the hotel a thorough once-over to ensure their safety before retiring herself. It was almost eight o'clock in the evening when they arrived and it was too dark to see everything inside. They were using the nineteen solar flashlights they had, spread amongst members of the construction team, to guide the hundreds of laborers down narrow hallways.

Colonel Harrison was the last one still standing. She had escorted the final group to the top floor and was making her way back down when she decided to scope out the hotel's common rooms for food and resources. Michigan's economy was on the rise right before the first pandemic hit in 2020.

Unfortunately, when things got tough and people turned violent, Michigan fell apart faster than any other State. The casinos were shut down, followed by the restaurants, and then the automotive plants. Lifelong residents suddenly headed south as gang violence resurged in the Detroit core. Many businesses were closed without warning and did not have any hope of re-opening.

Once back on the main floor, Amica scanned inside every door she passed. The first doors she entered were the public washrooms, where she found piles of toilet paper stacked high in a corner and a mixed match of hand and bar soaps scattered across the counters. The next door she opened was to a janitorial supply closet, also filled with random necessities. It appeared that at some point, someone was stockpiling supplies.

"Could that person still be inside?" She wondered out loud to herself.

The Colonel had people in every inch of the hotel, and they checked every room while assigning places to sleep. The only room they hadn't checked, besides the manager's office, was the kitchen attached to the hotel's surprisingly clean restaurant. There were at least two dozen team members sleeping in booths in the restaurant; Amica couldn't sleep until she knew the kitchen was empty.

She crept in slowly, trying not to disturb those resting, although a few were still sitting up, stretching out after the draining day's work. Amica gave them a reassuring nod and tiptoed towards the large metal swinging double doors. Armed with only her flashlight, she swung one side open with enough force that it instantly bounced back, slamming shut. It wasn't open long enough for her to get a good look inside. Now having spoiled the element of surprise, she slowly pushed open the door and slid inwards.

"Don't move," A deep voice commanded as she felt his wrist tightened around hers. "I have a gun."

The Colonel's backboned stiffened, using the tip of her elbow to confirm the location of her hidden switch blade. "I'm unarmed. Please don't shoot," Amica trembled back, intentionally allowing weakness to resonate in her voice, so the gunman wouldn't perceive her as a threat.

"Where did all these people come from?" The voice demanded.

"We are mostly Canadians. Are you from the United Resistors?"Amica inquired hopefully, in a hushed voice.

"I will ask the questions. How many people in your group have guns?" His voice was deep, though he kept the volume low enough not to startle those sleeping on the other side of the swing door.

"We come in peace. We don't want to harm you," Amica spoke softly with an elevated volume.

"Answer the question. How many guns? Where are your guns?" This time the man shouted into her face in a gruff Southern accent.

"We are unarmed." An admission the Colonel didn't want to make.

"How many people?" The voice demanded.

"There are a few hundred of us, spread out on every floor," She answered honestly.

"A few hundred people and no guns? Bullshit!" The stranger cocked his gun as he shouted.

"It's true, I assure you that we are a passive group." Amica placed her free hand on her heart in an attempt to signify her sincerity.

"You will never survive in Michigan if you're not armed." His volume decreased and his tone calmed somewhat as he continued, "Someone with you must have a gun."

"Sorry, sir, we have no guns. Canada banned all guns except a standard hunting rifle and no one has one here," She explained.

"This is my home and you're invading it. I'll give everyone five minutes to get out of here, leaving all of your supplies behind. Starting now!" He screamed his threat throughout the hushed space, pressing the nose of the gun against the tip of her nose.

"We're not causing you any harm. Please don't kick us out. If we promise not to take any of your supplies, can we leave first thing tomorrow," Amica pleaded, desperately trying to connect her eyes with his in the dark.

"If you want to stay, I can shoot you all in your sleep. Or you can be gone tonight." He quickly replied, still aiming the gun in Colonel Harrison's face.

All of a sudden, a bright blue light illuminated the center of the kitchen, startling Amica and the gun-toting stranger. Both blinked into the beam, trying to focus on the source. Tamika, a formidable Black woman with bulging biceps, was standing with one hand on her hip and the other on a massive LED flashlight.

She stared straight ahead at the source of the voice, a short, overweight, older man with an old-fashioned shotgun. Two men and another woman jumped to their feet next to her. A few more team members came into the kitchen from the dining area; several held solar lights that shone in the Colonel's direction.

"You don't have enough bullets for all of us, and if you kill one of us, the rest of us will jump on top of you before you get the next shot off. We're a team, an army, desperately trying to save this planet. You've never met a fighter more fierce than someone with a glimmer of hope in a hopeless world." Tamika's voice brought the bass needed to raise the rest of the room in unison as she walked toward the gunman with authority.

"We can offer you real hope, not hiding out in an abandoned building. We will share our supplies and help secure your home, but we're not giving up everything we have without a fight," The Colonel added, catching stride with Tamika.

The man fiddled with the gun, passing it back and forth. His eyes would connect with someone before his gaze quickly returned to the floor. He'd scratch his near-hairless scalp, looking directly at Tamika and squinting as if to size up his opponent. He would lift the gun towards Tamika, stare down the barrel of the gun, then flip it towards the ceiling, over and over in an internal debate about whether or not to pull the trigger. The Colonel was watching him carefully as her team eased in closer.

The man's eyes were noticeably red, which she assumed was either from a lack of sleep or too much alcohol. He couldn't stand still and was bumping into her as he fidgeted around. His clothing smelled like death, and she could see in his eyes that their begging wasn't penetrating his heart. Amica noticed his jaw was clenched as he lifted the gun once again, aiming directly at Tamika.

"Then you'll be the first to die." The stranger cocked the gun, pulling the trigger in one fluid motion.

The Colonel reacted instantly as the words were leaving his lips, knocking his forearm with enough power to tilt the gun towards the ceiling. The bullet whizzed by Tamika's ear, landing firmly in the wall behind her, a mere inch or two above her head. As the Colonel dove to tackle the perpetrator, the crowd swarmed in, and they were able to wrestle away his shotgun without further incident. Once he was held on the ground, Tamika sat down forcefully on the center of his back.

"Takes a lot more than a bullet to take me down, motherfucker," She snarled into his ear. "Colonel, looks like we gotta kill 'im now."

Colonel Harrison sighed, surveying the scene and assessing the current threat to her troops.

"The B.E.S.T. way is to create a society that does not tolerate any violence, and that includes us," Amica stated sternly, searching her mind for possible solutions.

"And when he kills one of us later on, will that still be the B.E.S.T. way?" Dylan, a burly handyman snarked his way into the discussion.

"I can respect your concerns, but there has to be a way that doesn't promote violence. We need to choose our actions wisely so that we can still live at peace with ourselves," The Colonel roared back with undeniable authority. Her usual moderate tone was kicked up a notch..

As she finished explaining her stance to the group surrounding her, Josée entered the room, marching with a man tied up next to her. His wrists and ankles were bound like prison shackles made from yellow vinyl rope.

"Found this scumbag lurking 'round the perimeter with a gun. Bullets have been removed and the weapon is now secure," Josée proudly reported. "How would you like me to dispose of him?"

The Colonel stared back blankly, deeply doubting her nonviolent strategies.

Garden of Eden

Back at the army base, there was more blossoming than just the vegetable gardens the team had planted. Ariel and Calvin were becoming increasingly close and moving closer with each explicit conversation. Her wicked innuendos while they were producing the wall pieces was inspiring Calvin's own erection poles. The manufacturing plant was a few hundred feet from the base, and there wasn't anyone else around once production wrapped up for the evening.

"It's impressive how many long poles we've formed in only a matter of days." Ariel said suggestively, while stroking the smooth dark gray plastic, teasing Calvin with each glide of her hand.

"We're pumping them out so fast that we're almost out of rubber tires to hold them in place." Ariel continued with a devious smile, "What else could we use that has a hole big enough to wrap around our erection poles?"

Calvin didn't have enough blood to his brain to provide any intelligible answer, mustering a wide-eyed shrug instead, accompanied by a quiet moan.

"These are the biggest poles I've ever seen. They are just waiting to be shoved into the hole, so they can stand solid like a rock, protecting us from any nastiness trying to force its way in." Ariel's subtle innuendos were obliterated in filth, as she slid towards him, bridging any physical distance left between them.

Ariel pressed her body firmly up against his, and could feel his approval pushing through his loose track pants. He leaned in and slowly whispered "Yessss" into her ear. His warm breath sent tingles down her liquified core.

Neither could deny the sexual tension that had been escalating for days and now was their chance. Ariel's hand slipped from her waist, casually dancing her fingertips along his balls before settling on his enlarged cock. "I guess the poles are not the only thing solid as a rock."

Calvin let a groan escape, still unable to form words. It had been months since he had sex with someone and was beginning to wonder if it'd ever happen again. His sexuality wasn't fluid, strictly attracted to the female form and believed in the values of commitment. Monogamy was a dying concept and it was becoming increasingly harder to find a woman who wanted to settle down with only one man.

Ariel stood back and untied the drawstring holding up her comfy, cotton pants. They fell gracefully down to her ankles within seconds, exposing a hint of her little black thong just below where her shirt touched her thighs.

Calvin hoisted Ariel onto the massive metal slab they used to sort through recyclable for raw material. It was usually quite filthy, but had just been thoroughly scrubbed with disinfectant by the budding couple at the end of their shift. Both were so revved up, that it wouldn't have mattered.

"I've wanted your hands on my body for weeks." Ariel whispered, well aware of the effect her forwardness was having on her new lover.

Calvin moaned loudly, gliding her thong down her body as she wiggled free. He pulled Ariel closer to him, until their bodies were connected. She returned the moan, using her hips to propel him deeper inside.

Ariel rode his hard body, gripping onto his shoulders and thrashing loudly as her bottom bounced on the cold steel. Calvin and Ariel's physical intimacy felt natural, somewhat inevitable.The sexual tension and desire to get closer had been escalating for weeks; an explosion was imminent.

Their first heated encounter was a few weeks prior, shortly after the majority of team members had left to build the wall. They were on a day trip to look for affordable food supplies to restock the pantry and salvage yards that would donate scrap tires to their cause. They mapped out six stops and left together in the Colonel's borrowed Cargo POP at seven am.

Personal Operational Planes became popular after the oil crisis caused by the nuclear wars in the Middle East. They were solar-powered engines that could make about one hundred miles on a fully-charged battery and were nearly limitless when there was not a cloud in the sky. The downfalls were that it could not safely fly higher than twelve feet or travel faster than fifty miles per hour. The entire casing of the mini plane was coated with a thick bubble foam to cushion the impact in case of a crash, and then painted with silicone solar coating.

Although the wings expanded to both twelve and twenty-four feet wide depending on your altitude, they folded back down using two sets of brass hinges. The flexible mechanical design allowed the wings to remain stationary when required to soar longer distances or spin to hover over a space. Once the plane had safely landed, the wings were stored on top of the plane's six-foot-wide egg-shaped body. The stationary plane didn't take up any more room than a classic Sports Utility Vehicle.

However, there was not much room inside the narrow POP cockpit, so Ariel and Calvin's hands kept brushing up against one another. The air was humid, thick with smog, and both stripped off their top layer immediately after exiting the POP once they arrived at the first Superstore.

Every store had buying limits on the most sought-after essentials due to depleted supplies. Their strategy was to search for less popular items that were still rich in nutrients. The team had planted several acres of vegetables and wheat, but it would take time for their crops to flourish enough to feed the masses. They sent almost all of the food they gathered during the first few weeks on the road with the border wall construction team. The pantry was bare.

Royelle had promised a truckload of meals with the next shipment of wall posts, which was expected to leave the base in four days. They currently only had one cup of hummus, ten homemade toast points, five strawberries, and one mini cucumber per team member. Royelle was going to use the overripe bananas, frozen blueberries, honey, granola, and almond butter they had left over to make protein bars while Calvin and Ariel scavenged the Great Toronto Area for more substantial meal ideas.

Their rusted shopping cart currently contained two large jars of pickled beets, two heads of iceberg lettuce, one three pack of romaine lettuce, three cucumbers, three green peppers, three sweet potatoes, one bag of spanish onions, two bags of raw kidney beans, one bottle of vinegar, one bottle of olive oil, two containers of feta cheese, a small brick of cheddar cheese, and a large tin of canned corn.

For the vegetables and cheese, these were the maximum quantities they could purchase and there were very few other options at the first store. The total for the four bags of groceries was one hundred and eighty-six Canadian dollars. Global companies collapsed during the war due to a lack of human and material resources. Most of the superstore's produce was locally grown, driving costs up.

The next place they stopped at was a survival shop that carried a wide range of unusual items. They picked up two dozen solar batteries, six flashlights, two long ropes, a box of mesh bandaging, a box of one ounce storage bottles, a box of five thousand paper lunch bags, and a box of five hundred small reusable containers. They also grabbed two bags of dehydrated banana chips and two bags of apple cinnamon chips at the counter. Their small haul was just over eight hundred and sixty dollars.

The third stop was a junkyard that had a few truckloads' worth of old tires. They were more than happy to donate the entire lot. The owner hadn't seen anyone in days and the two men jauntily conversed for an hour while Ariel listened patiently. After they left, Calvin arranged for a few transports to pick up the tires the following morning. Ariel admired his ease with strangers and his sweet attempts to include her in their conversation about cars and the collapse of the automotive industry, even if it put them behind schedule.

Their fourth stop was a farmer-organized market set up within a parking lot. It had a wooden sign advertising fresh fruits and vegetables in bright orange letters. This time they scored four heads of iceberg lettuce, five green peppers, three sweet potatoes, two bags of beets, one bag of spanish onions, one pound of carrots, a dozen bananas, four green apples, two bags of dried oregano, a bottle of lemon juice, and two dozen eggs. They now had everything they needed to make a large Greek salad and divide it into containers for the road crew. They were praying Royelle could work magic with the rest of their groceries.

The fifth stop was a used car dealership that had sixty unwanted old tires. Calvin arranged for them to go on the last load from the junkyard, hoping they would fit without sending a separate truck. Calvin poured on his usual charm and the owner sent them away with an additional three pounds of grapes from his personal vineyard.

"This is so generous! Grapes are hard to find; we've been to two stores already today and they were completely sold out," Ariel gushed.

"I have acres of grapes. I trade them with other locals for various crops. It keeps us fed," Emmitt, the kind-eyed salesman, stated.

"We're actually launching a community project where we pool our resources to rebuild this world and help the environment, as well as each other. Would that interest you and your neighbors?" Ariel eagerly asked..

"Absolutely. I'm not sure how I can help, but I'll trade grapes for just about anything. I used to love them, but it's all my wife and I eat anymore," Emmitt pointed to his farmhouse at the back, where they assumed his wife must be.

"We planted fields of lettuce, tomatoes, cucumbers, peppers, and green beans. I'm sure we will have enough to send some your way in a few weeks," Ariel answered.

"Here, I'll give you my contact info and we can work out the details when we get back to base camp." Calvin clicked his wristband to activate the contact remittance app, connected virtual faces with Emmitt's band, and their contact information was transmitted to one another's data file.

"It was nice to meet both of you. You're a lovely couple, and are welcome to dine with me and my lady next time you're out this way," Emmitt offered.

"That would be lovely." Ariel patted her chest in a gesture that showed her sincerity, pretending to ignore his assumption that they were a couple. There was no need to correct him; it was already feeling like an intimate relationship without ever physically being affectionate towards one another.

After saying their goodbyes, the pair hopped back inside the POP to glide onto their next destination. Although POPs were gaining in popularity, they were slow, couldn't soar above tall buildings, and rarely had smooth landings. The benefit was not having to drive on the cracked roadways that were long overdue to be repaved.

Toronto was one of the few cities in Canada that still had over one million people living in it (according to the last census in 2036), however it once exceeded six million people. The drastic drop in residents was evident by the quiet streets, wide open highways, and ample parking spots. Their next short trip was also quiet, until Calvin broke the silence.

"That was smart recruiting Emmitt once you heard about his vineyard and food trading. I like a woman who can think on her feet."

B.E.S.T.

The words he was mulling over in his head finally seeped out after setting the bubble plane down as gently as possible.

"Thank you. That was an excellent landing. You're a pretty smooth operator as well," Ariel fired back with a suggestive eyebrow raise.

"I get the job done," He suggestively implied with a giddy, boyish wink.

"I bet you do."

She stared deep into his eyes, her body felt as if it was being pulled in towards his solid chest. Just as Calvin leaned in to meet her halfway, Ariel pulled herself away, announcing awkwardly to the windshield of the plane, "Alright, let's hop to it. This is our last chance not to let a few thousand people starve."

"I saw a farm with a large market stand in front of it on the flight here. We can check there as well. Don't worry, we'll come through for the team. No one will starve on our watch." Ariel's sudden rejection didn't seem to phase him; his gut knew there would be another chance.

Calvin gave her hand a quick squeeze and then ventured into a local market together, oddly located where the former financial district once stood. Unfortunately, this time they only picked up one bunch of overripe bananas, two pints of cherry tomatoes, one head of romaine, four cans of tuna, a pint of blueberries, and a one-pound bag of dried cranberries.

"We came too late in the day. Everything's been picked over," Ariel sighed as they headed back towards their plane. "We'll know better for next time."

"Every inch of the POP is packed, including the cargo bag strapped underneath. We couldn't fit any more food if we had found it. We did good, Ariel." His kind eyes reassured her with every word.

"I just can't imagine that this will give us enough to feed the troops who are doing all of that hard labor, building a wall to keep us safe." Ariel's concern was legitimate, but she was trying to arrange another excursion together.

"Royelle will make it work, and if not, at least everyone still has nutritional supplements to get them through. No one will starve to death." Calvin was still not catching on to her hidden agenda.

"Or maybe we can try to find more again, sometime soon? Today was a fun adventure. Can't we go on another resource excursion together, maybe in the near future?" Ariel was done playing coy and emphasized the word *together.*

"You've got a date! In fact, I'm free tomorrow," Calvin exclaimed, biting his lip in anticipation.

That supply trip inspired many more, and they would eagerly team up with one another on every task at the base. In only a matter of weeks, the filthy innuendos and suggestive caressing were escalating with every encounter and neither wanted to hold back when the fire reached its peak on the packing counter. Their friendly flirting was now a passionate inferno ready to explode.

Ariel was nineteen in 2039 and convinced the world would not last until her twenty-first birthday. As the bleak outlook of her future progressed prior to meeting the Colonel, Ariel lost interest in pursuing all forms of romantic love. Passion felt pointless and she poured herself into obtaining online medical and environmental degrees. It had been over a year since she felt the hands of a man on her skin. B.E.S.T. had given her a reason to love life and experience physical connection again.

Incarceration Situation

Josée's steely stare drilled into the Colonel's heart as her mind flooded with gruesome memories from detaining captures in the third world war. The threat seemed quite certain, as the two men exchanged a look indicating they were familiar with one another, before glancing back towards the floor. The Colonel paced between their two captures, grasping at the air for an answer to their current predicament.

"I can't allow them to be killed, nor can we risk setting them free. Josée, Tamika, Arturo, let's bring these men to a room where we can discuss potential solutions in private. Jarrod, Dylan, Oliver, and Bella, please pair up and patrol the rest of the perimeter. It seems we are not the only ones who want to rest here tonight," The Colonel commanded.

"I understand that it won't be easy, but everyone should try to get some sleep. There's hard work to be done tomorrow and we need you to be at your best." Colonel Harrison made eye contact with as many people in the room as possible, trying to assure them that she would keep them safe.

Amica scoped out the main floor, looking for any signs of an office that could house a hackable security system. Although there was currently no power in the building, they did have several charged generators on their transport trucks.

If this hotel was a gathering place for vagrant Americans, then working security cameras could really come in handy. The Colonel recalled two rooms off the front desk that had windowless doors. She motioned in their direction, and Arturo led the women and the men they captured inside the first room.

"Push those chairs into opposing corners and please tie these gents up securely." The Colonel's mind was still developing a plan of action, as she directed her team step by step. Amica knew bad guys were a possibility and had more experience than she wanted to admit in torture, even killing, in the name of war. She promised herself B.E.S.T.'s attempt at utopia would be different.

After tying up her prisoner extra tightly, Josée skipped over to the Colonel with a grin. "Interrogate and then eliminate?"

"I still feel that we can handle this in a better way. I understand you, Josée. You and I have similar training, but I want to challenge you to think outside the box. They are human beings who are only fighting for their survival, just like we are doing," Amica appealed to her new friend's compassion.

"And if they kill you in that fight?" She fired back fiercely.

"What if we relocate them somewhere else instead, a place where we could put all the violent predators permanently?" The Colonel couldn't suppress a smirk when she realized she was staring at the first two residents of the 'Badlands' in Australia.

"So we're building a prison?" Josée guessed, squinting her eyes in search of other possibilities.

"Yeah, but more along the lines of Alcatraz. Once we determine that these are the only two threats in the area, Arturo and I will take them back to base camp and hold them somewhere secure. I'll need to check on Prime Minister Cortez's progress with the next phase of our mission, but she should be almost ready," Amica explained to herself while further confusing Josée.

"Ready for what?" Josée asked.

"It looks like we will now need to accelerate the evacuation plans and make a temporary room for our unexpected guests in the meantime. I promise we will ship them off as soon as we can do so safely." The Colonel's deliciously devious smile when she finished talking was enough to reassure Josée enough to stop her from asking any additional questions.

Jarrod and Bella reported back first, saying that they had circled the exterior of the building twice with no sign of life. Dylan and Oliver took the elevator to the top floor and slowly trotted down the stairs, stopping to check each room on each level, before concluding that only their community members were sleeping inside the hotel.

The eight chosen soldiers took turns for the remainder of the night, alternating guard, patrol, and sleep in three-hour shifts. Two teammates guarded the men strapped to chairs in the office, two patrolled the entrances on the main floor, while the other four slept on the floor of the office next door.

The Colonel knew that although they may have survived the night without another encounter, it wouldn't be long before some wild gunman threatened their lives again. It was now or never. Her plan to drive the most dangerous and self-serving people to Australia and then strand them there forever (or until they killed themselves off) was the inevitable next step in her plan to save the world.

Holy fuck, Amica's brain screamed from the inside, *This is actually going to happen.* Her plan was just crazy enough that it could work, yet so crazy that their entire team could end up dying if it didn't. It was Amica's turn to take a break from security detail, but only her body lay still, paralyzed by fear. Her mind was rehearsing every detail of the misinformation campaign, searching for safeguards to ensure the intended outcome.

First thing the following morning, the Colonel gathered Antonio, Sarah, and Doctor Martin to go over the intended route to Chicago, She instructed them to work together as team leaders, with Doctor Martin being the tiebreaker if ever required. Colonel Harrison then spoke with Tamika and Dylan about taking on the role of security, and asked Bella to manage the food distribution for the construction site.

Josée insisted on riding in the back of the truck with both bound prisoners before Colonel Harrison could officially assign her a duty. She was proving herself to be a fearless and valuable asset, willing to risk her life to protect the masses. Amica knew Josée's skills would be required in the next phase, and was happy to keep her close by.

The Colonel had paid close attention to those around her during both their caravan-style travels to the most southern point of Canada and during the laborious tasks of constructing the wall in Michigan. She made a mental note of those who were focused on helping others above themselves: those who could be trusted to do the right thing when no one was looking. She listened closely to hear who the true encouragers and leaders were, and who complained or wandered off.

Trust and confidentiality would be critical to the success of their division campaign, and being social media savvy was just as necessary. The Colonel mentally finalized her new team list while riding shotgun on the ride back to base camp.

Arturo, Prime Minister Felicia Cortez, Commander Mei Ying, Kali Robbins, Josée, Tamika, and Royelle had her trust She also wrote down Jarrod "Knows Shows" Parker, a retired Marine and popular political activist on social media who had over one hundred thousand like-minded followers. He seemed willing to do whatever was asked of him to build the wall and was a known activist for better gun control after witnessing the devastation guns caused in the midst of World War III.. Amica added beauty blogger Jodi at the end, due to her impressive social media presence and genuine interest in the project.

Her next task was figuring out somewhere to secure their prisoners until the vessels arrived at the ports in Vancouver and the water's edge of where the state of Florida once existed. The Colonel mentally scanned every inch of the army base, trying to find an area that would be easy to patrol, yet nowhere near the rest of the team's housing. The base had several airplane hangars, including one with an old Boeing B-52 that crashed decades ago, blowing all of its engines and destroying its landing gear. The massive plane had been gutted and striped for parts. The rusted shell was hollow and easy to secure.

"Arturo, do you think we can use the old B-52 as a holding cell for a few weeks?" Amica asked her assistant, and valued colleague's opinion.

"It's big enough to hold them and we can ensure that there is only one way in or out. There's also plenty of room outside the plane within the hangar to set up additional foot patrols." Arturo nodded with each fact. "It's definitely a viable choice, Colonel, especially since it is permanently stationary."

"Well, it has no engine and one wing, so I don't see it going anywhere fast," Amica teased. "We'll take them straight there when we get back until we can relocate them to a permanent home."

"You're going to lock us up?" One of the bound men questioned from the backseat.

"Yes," Amica responded calmly without hesitation.

"We can be of service. We won't cause you any trouble," The other man pleaded.

"Don't make us prisoners," The first man added.

"Unfortunately, in our brief introduction earlier, you both proved that we can't trust you if we don't keep you somewhere secure." The Colonel was firm in her resolve that any civilian who threatened violence could no longer be left to their own free will.

Her experiences in the Canadian army gave her a crash course about how violence was used to assert control and power. The first unit she was assigned was led by an almost criminal psychopath who got off on torturing his team into submission. In the very first week, he took the team out for a sixteen-mile trek through rough terrain, wearing backpacks that were weighed down with forty pounds of rocks. It was thirty-eight degrees Celsius.

They were approximately twelve miles in and the burning pain in Amica's shoulders was too much for her to continue ignoring it. Although she had solid arm and shoulder muscles, her frame was too petite to manage the additional burden. Her sweat increased the friction, tearing the strap into her flesh. She tried to discreetly stop and remove it for a moment, but Commander Flemming noticed immediately.

"Keep going, Private Harrison." His tone was firm and unwavering.

"I believe the bag is cutting into my skin. I just need to readjust," She stammered.

"You can remove it in four more miles; not a second sooner," The formidable commander insisted.

When they returned to base, the gash in both her shoulders was so wide it required several stitches to stay closed. After learning that Amica required stitches, Commander Flemming decided she needed additional climbs wearing the weighted sack to strengthen her muscles and toughen her skin, but it only further destroyed her fragile flesh. The scars are still noticeable: a reminder of his cruelty.

In the battle against American rebel forces, Amica witnessed Commander Flemming snap a man's neck after he relinquished his gun. He encouraged physical combat within the team and turned a blind eye when soldiers raped captives. He insisted violence was the only answer, and more than a decade later, this was Amica's chance to prove him wrong.

When they returned to base, they brought the two prisoners to the old hanger, fed them the same meal as everyone else, and then secured them to chairs inside the broken-down bomber using ropes and chain wound within one another. Josée proudly volunteered for the first shift guarding the prisoners.

The Colonel found several other laborers working on the wall production to patrol the area every thirty minutes. She had to ensure they were protected on this side of the world before taking the risks involved with the next part of her plan. Their plans for building a new world were no longer a safe secret kept amongst lifelong friends.

The Colonel made the conscientious decision to get a good night's rest first, and then she would arrange an emergency meeting for the following evening with the new team. Prime Minister Cortez was still in Australia finalizing the shipments and recruiting more team members. Several members would need to be pulled off the construction team to help with their next mission. Everything was happening faster than she could keep up with.

In the morning, she communicated with each person through coded email and virtual chats that plans were taking a big leap forward. She asked Commander Ying, Kali, Jarrod, and Jodi to return from Michigan, explaining in a video chat only that she needed their help to pull off phase two. Amica would save the sordid details for when they could gather in a secure room together.

Misinformation Campaign

"Welcome to the B.E.S.T. elite misinformation squad. The nine of you were selected for a very special and incredibly secretive mission. The details I'm about to share cannot be repeated outside of this circle. Our success hinges on keeping the core purpose of the campaign confidential. Please speak up now if you have any concerns that you won't be able to keep this secret completely to yourself."

The Colonel made eye contact with each individual team member, allowing for several seconds of silence to pass before continuing on.

"Our greatest potential for failure in rebuilding a better world comes from the entitled rebels controlling the New United Republic and North State Communities. They are using intimidation and violence to ruin everything worth saving. The walls we are building to secure our new border is only the first step in ensuring our safety." Colonel Harrison paused to take a deep breath before jumping into the riskiest part of her plan.

"The most dangerous people have money and selfish interests. We can use their egos and greed to our advantage." Her eyes twinkled, revealing the evil genius that lay stagnant within her soul. Amica dated a very affluent narcissist in college who used to think he could buy his way out of anything. She relished the thought of how he was likely to get sucked into their scam.

"What if we put all the bad guys in one place, far away from here?" She questioned the group, seeing smiles on Royelle and Kali's faces, who knew where the conversation was headed.

No one answered out loud, although some nodded along at the suggestion. Amica could see calm in the eyes of those who already knew and confusion from those who weren't previously tipped off by prior discussions. "Arturo, can you please pass out the campaign packets?

"The campaign flyers inside this envelope will be transferred to you as well, using the separate connect accounts we've set up on your behalf. Any communication regarding this project must be done using the encrypted account specified in your assigned packets.

"Our goal is to distribute this information online anywhere that we can, from as many accounts as you can create. You'll notice the two campaigns we are pushing out to the public are very different from one another. I only want one or the other shared per site. If it's a liberal-minded, environmentally-conscientious or anti-violence group, please share the campaign to bring more recruits to B.E.S.T. If the site's content is geared towards the outlaws or southern rebels, please share the Australian campaign." The rehearsed words slipped from her lips in a monotone.

The room was void of noise as each person read over the documents they were just handed. The first document was a one-page flyer with bold, gold highlights emphasizing select trigger words. There was a pink sticky note at the top that read:

"For Rebel and NRA sponsored News Outlets."
$150,000 will save your life!

The New United Republic is crumbling quickly. Natural resources are scarce and dangerous immigrants from South America are invading through Mexico to steal what we have left. Australia still has ample vegetation and wildlife, but few people are currently residing there. Most Australians moved to the former United States, Canada, and Europe prior to WWIII, when the mainland was destroyed by bushfires and sinking shorelines.

Australians invaded us and now it's our turn!

The lack of human interference gave the rainforests a chance to flourish and wild pigs can be seen in large groups throughout the countryside. There hasn't been a bush fire in years and the coast is shrinking faster in North America than it is in Australia.

Do you deserve to be **one of the chosen few** who will survive the rapture?

If you have the financial means, there is still hope for your future. Commander RJ Reynolds is a former Navy Seal with the resources and strategy to survive these dark times. He is organizing three vessels of supplies and passengers to travel from the former Florida coastline to Australia, beginning on September first.

There is only room for nine hundred people: three hundred per ship. All meals will be supplied and we will have cargo storage for any personal effects. This opportunity is only for the elite and reservations start at one hundred and fifty thousand dollars per person. There will also be thirty luxury rooms available for two hundred thousand dollars per person per ship. If we receive more than nine hundred requests, the Commander will narrow the field based on financial, educational, and heredity qualifications. Anyone with a history of opposing the NUR rights and freedoms charter or protested against the NRA during the civil war will not be welcome on this ship.

We only want the best and the brightest in our new world order.

Commander Reynolds has a team of experts currently constructing two hundred and fifty homes around the base of Mount Kosciuszko. These weatherproof, two-bedroom, fifteen hundred square foot units will be available for an additional two hundred and fifty thousand dollars paid in advance. The Commander hired the most qualified agriculturalists to revive the forests and create fields full of fresh vegetables and fruit. The first crops will be ready for harvesting by the time the boat arrives in late September.

There is another ship *en route* to Australia carrying sixteen cows, eighteen pigs and fifty-two chickens for breeding and future consumption. You can purchase a personal servant to harvest, slaughter, and prepare your bounty for an additional fifty thousand once we arrive. Commander Reynolds is our saving Grace for those who can afford his blessings.

Travel Regulations:

Passengers are allowed two suitcases and two firearms per person. All ammunition will be in a locked safe under the Commander's control until we arrive in Australia. There will be a large storage space in the hull of the boat for non-perishable food items. Please bring any resources you can access, as a return trip has not been scheduled. Time and location details will be given once payment has been made in full.

Please contact Constance Reeves at 599-614-1984 to book your spot **ASAP!**

These ships will fill fast and there won't be another opportunity to escape our crumbling country. **Are you worthy of being saved?**

The second sheet of paper was a plain typed sheet that had a short email address at the top and a longer one at the bottom. The pink note adhered to it specified **"Liberal and Environmental Conscience News Outlets."**

Fellow Humanitarians,

If you still have hope, we have a plan. Colonel Amica Harrison is searching for hard-working, big-hearted people to help repair environmental damage and rebuild a civilized society. Located in the heart of Canada, we're creating a unified, socially-conscientious utopia within a secure environment. This new world has real potential for growth and prosperity.

We're looking for good people who are willing to share their resources and work on rebuilding a sustainable world. If that sounds like something you can get behind, please message the Colonel through the B.E.S.T. APP link and provide your contact connect profile. We will then show you how you can help us save the world before it's too late.

**AUTOMATIC EMAIL RESPONSE
WELCOME TO B.E.S.T.**

Our world can be saved through Balance, Equity, Sustainability, and Teamwork. To ensure the new world gets off on the right foot, we need your commitment to the nine rules set forth by our founding members. If you can sincerely commit to the following terms and conditions, please sign and send back.

The B.E.S.T. Community Commitment

Established July eighteenth, 2041

1. Violence of any kind will result in immediate expulsion from B.E.S.T.
2. All guns and automatic weaponry is outlawed in B.E.S.T.
3. Pesticides, tobacco, and opioids are illegal and usage will result in expulsion.
4. Every person over the age of sixteen must grow and contribute at least one crop in bulk to the team, plus one outdoor tree

and a minimum of three houseplants, using recycled, purified rainwater.

5. Every person between the age of sixteen and nineteen must work ten hours per week.

6. Every person twenty years or older must work thirty hours per week until age sixty-five. Work will be catered to each individual's skill set and physical capabilities. Everyone must be willing to do something that benefits more than just themselves.

7. Reuse, reduce, and recycle must be practiced at all times. Fines will be issued for abuse of natural or limited resources.

8. All food will be rationed and divided equally amongst all members

9. Every person is equal to everyone else and no person shall be discriminated against or given special treatment for any reason.

To create a balanced, equitable, sustainable team environment, everyone is asked to take the above pledge seriously. Anyone found breaking the established rules will be immediately expelled from the B.E.S.T. utopia community. Once you become a member, you are able to challenge a rule or ruling through a virtual vote where every member will be given the opportunity to weigh in. We will work as a team, and we will win as a team.

Sincerely,
Colonel Amica Harrison

Colonel Harrison watched their reactions carefully, waiting for everyone to look away from the papers before continuing on. The wide eyes and toothy grins greeting her allowed a sigh of relief to escape.

"In addition to the specific campaigns we've created to recruit more members for the B.E.S.T. team and the other to drive those unwilling to work into the 'Badlands' of Australia, we will also have a few supporting articles to nudge each person in the right direction.

"In conspiracy news outlets and gun enthusiast publications, we will be sharing various stories about Ontario sinking into the Great Lakes and wildfires in Algonquin park. I wrote a few articles implying world treasures are being stored on Mount Kosciuszko in Australia and

Canadian activists are flying wild animals to Australia to keep them safe from poachers," The Colonel continued.

"Is any of that true?" Jodi interrupted Amica's rehearsed speech.

"Quite the opposite, truthfully. As we speak, Prime Minister Cortez and her team are gathering all transportable resources in Australia onto ships destined for the West Coast. We will then send three Canadian vessels to the Tallahesse shoreline to pick up those who bought into our relocation campaign," The Colonel explained.

"How can you be certain the right people will end up in the right place?" Tamika asked.

The Colonel sighed too loudly to hide, as this was a question she was continually asking herself.

"Although there are no guarantees, it should divide people at their core. Those who are willing to work, are against violence, and want to rebuild the earth the right way, I assume, will be motivated to join our team. Those who value money and guns above all else should be enticed onto the ship. It has its flaws and we won't know if it'll even work until we try. But wouldn't that be true with any plan at this point? We are up against utter chaos." A nervous chuckle slipped from her throat between the last two sentences.

"How can you keep everyone in Australia?" Jarrod jumped into the conversation.

"It's a one-way ticket. Prime Minister Cortez is making sure there are no planes or sea-worthy vessels left in Australia before these ships arrive. Once the boat is docked, only the Captain and our crew will return." Amica appreciated the questions, but kept going with her planned discussion before anyone else could interject. "We need this information to circulate everywhere, and quickly. However, it is essential that no one knows who is spreading it or why."

Stressing the secrecy once more, she added, "The misinformation campaign can only be successful if everyone reading it believes both scenarios to be true. Do I have your support and assurance that everything we discussed today will be kept confidential?"

Her words sounded confident, but Amica's palms were damp and her fingers trembled at her side. Relief calmed her as the team began nodding in agreement.

"Always," Royelle was the first to respond, loudly and eagerly.

"I'd rather stick all the murderous assholes on a boat and blow it up, but I get the need for a clean conscience. I'm in," Josée flew to her feet and replied with a formal salute.

"Yes. I honestly think it could work. Myself and the remaining community of Asia that I represent give you the discrete and complete support of our resources," Commander Ming pledged her commitment.

"Now I know why I was chosen. This is payback for the 2016 election and I love it. Count me in," Jarrod Parkers said with a wide grin.

"I still have a lot of followers and will do whatever I can to help spread the word," Amanda added, while Kali nodded enthusiastically alongside her.

"Take tonight to review both documents and let me know if you have any changes or suggestions. We'll start tomorrow morning in a scattered approach, focusing first on the campaign to bring in more recruits. Arturo will send a distribution schedule with the files. If you have any questions, you can reach out to me directly," Amica raced through the closing of her prepared speech and finished with a loud exhale.

Heads bobbing up and down cascaded in front of her, as the misinformation team gathered their belongings and said their goodbyes. Royelle lingered to check in on her lifelong friend.

"How do you feel now that this is all actually happening?" She asked sincerely.

"Terrified," The words slipped from Amica's lips without filtering herself to sound confident. Her heart was still racing.

"I would guess so, but you shouldn't be. This is the only plan anyone has believed in for years and you've convinced an army we can fix this broken world. Don't start doubting yourself now." Royelle's kind words were accompanied by a stern look.

"I know," She replied in an almost inaudible hush.

"And I will be here to remind you," Royelle quickly added while grabbing Amica for a tight hug.

This wasn't the first time Royelle had given Amica a necessary peptalk, nor would it be the last. Amica was also ready to quit after her first few weeks in the army. Besides the physical abuse of her commander, the constant sexual innuendos and harassment was wearing her down. Her firm rejections and attempts to stick up for herself weren't being taken seriously.

Amica called Royelle late one night during a crying fit, fighting the urge to scream and smash every inch of the tiny bathroom stall she was hiding inside. It was almost lights out, and it was the only place she could find to talk privately.

"I need to come home. I'm not strong enough to make the cut," She stammered between sobs.

"You're capable of handling anything you set your mind to do. Why do you really want to come home?" Royelle fired back with a snap.

"Fucking macho pricks won't ever shut up! They taunt you at every step and push you to do physically impossible shit. Plus, everything I do is followed by a comment about how my tits must get in the way or how my breasts will protect me in battle. I'm going to end up shooting someone on our side. I can't grin and bear it any longer. I'm done, Royelle." Amica's volume raised with each word, no longer caring if someone wandered by and overheard her confession.

"Since when do remarks like that get under your skin? Ignore the stupid nonsense they say, but pay close attention to their actions. That's the advice you've always given me. Be aloof and alert," Royelle replied, calm and collected.

"It gets worse if I compete at their level. I beat some ass in a training drill and he fucking body-checked me down a flight of stairs. He acted like it was an accident and then showed me his teeth. It was intentional. He's lucky I only got a few bruises and a broken finger." Her rant continued to spew in frustration.

"I assume he received a few rough shots in return?" Royelle asked.

"Sadly, no. I did nothing so I wouldn't further provoke him," Amica reluctantly admitted after a moment of silence.

"What the fuck, Amica? Since when do you tolerate that shit? Look at everything you've accomplished by not backing down when it matters. Don't let anyone discourage you from achieving what you set out to do," Royelle relentlessly drilled into her, as all best friends should do when the other's confidence is teetering.

She was right ten years ago and probably right again now. Amica knew that no matter how many times she tried to talk herself out of making the necessary next step, it was the only option they had left. The two lifelong friends agreed to meet after Amica's morning run so they could hit send on the first batch of emails simultaneously. Royelle understood that Amica had the weight of the world on her shoulders and volunteered to share some of the load. The next few days would determine how their role played out in the history books.

Or if there would ever be a new book on history.

Battle on Every Front

It was only the third day of the B.E.S.T. team flooding social media with both the recruitment and misinformation campaigns and new recruits were signing up by the hundreds! Kali and Arturo put together a separate team to vet and track the new member requests. The group lovingly referred to as the HR Squad reviewed each person's online presence to ensure they were a compatible member and then assessed which workstream they could benefit the most.

On the other hand, Commander Reeves's sales pitch had only secured seventeen spots on the ship to the 'Badlands.' They received a few dozen inquiries from people that weren't ready to commit and recorded those individuals' names as being possibly ineligible for B.E.S.T., just in case they applied later out of desperation.

Some accounts were flagged due to sending nasty message alerts to the Colonel's recruitment account. Most were harmless responses, except several threatening DMs from the same vague account, biggunbegun@gmail.com. The person sent a threat to the recruitment portal's account, which was automatically set up to forward the auto response listing the B.E.S.T. rules.

The human being hiding behind "big gun be gun" sent two identical messages three times in a row.

Communist Socialist Bitch—Your new world won't work. People don't want to work and the environment is fucked. Stop exploiting people with fake dreams.

Sincerely, a real soldier.

The second message arrived in response to the team contract and it was just as concerning.

Correction, Foolish Communist Socialist Bitch! No one is dumb enough to sign this contract. You're not a threat to our freedom. You're a joke.

Sincerely, YOUR Commander

Colonel Harrison's friend at Google and his team searched online for any connection of that handle, but it wasn't linked to any identifiable human. It could be a troll bot programmed to repeat a cycle of emails at random intervals. Even if the sender wasn't a physical entity, the person creating and controlling the bot must have been. Unfortunately, the Colonel didn't have much time to fret over the online threat because a physical one was trying to undo all of their work to secure utopia.

Antonio called from the front line when the crew encountered a militia in Rockford, Illinois. They had guns and were threatening to take the team's recently replenished food supply, tools, and equipment. Three larger men from the wall-building team surrounded the six men and two women aiming handguns in every direction. More than a dozen other B.E.S.T. team members filed in behind them, hoping their sheer numbers would prevent anyone from firing.

"You're outnumbered," Blake, a burly six-foot-three man said sternly, staring down the barrel of the closest man's gun. "You start shooting and we start swinging. Next thing you know, it's a pile of dead bodies, including yours. Go on your side of the wall and let us continue along our way, and everyone lives."

"You can't start building a wall in the middle of our city and think we're going to stand back and allow it." The aggressor shoved his gun into Blake's chin.

"We'll leave your section of the city alone. We're heading back north anyway and will be out of your way by the end of the day. We're not giving up our rations without a fight, but this doesn't need to turn ugly," Blake calmly reasoned with the man.

"No one wants people dying and maybe we won't steal your shit, but we sure as fuck are not letting you push us on that side of the wall. We were here first. Your wall is on our land." The two men's noses were inches from one another, neither willing to back down.

"You can have everything on the other side once we finish putting the wall up here." Sarah moved next to Blake, as she was never one to back down from a fight.

"Pretty sure you don't own this land, pretty little lady." The toothless gent who smelled like he hadn't used soap in years attempted to stare down the less-intimidating, much sweeter-smelling architect. As the aggressor leaned in towards Sarah, big bad Beth-Anne pushed her way into the pack to back up Blake and Sarah. At six-foot-two and two hundred and twenty pounds of solid muscle, B-A was far from little.

"We do now," B-A answered for the team, puffing her chest up to prove she could hold her own.

Antonio, a short but physically fit man, ducked behind his team to relay the conversation and current situation to the Colonel. He wanted her advice before proceeding. "I know we're against using violence, but there are eight guns pointed at us and someone will get hurt if we don't do something."

"It seems you've already solved it. It's not about robbing you of supplies; they don't want the wall built in Rockford. Tell them you'll reroute towards Milwaukee, head north-west until they are long out of your sight, and then go east towards Minnesota. We might lose some space, but if it keeps them away, it's worth the small sacrifice."

"We've already put up some of the wall on what they claim is their land," Antonio clarified.

"If they insist we move it, then we can pull it up and replant those pieces. The cement shouldn't have solidified already. Let's try to keep the peace first, because I have no idea where the closest working hospital may be. The team's safety is the first priority, always."

"Thank you, Colonel. I'll let you know how it goes."

Antonio forced himself back into the center of the crowd, holding one arm in the air, waving frantically. "Please, please, may I have your attention? I have a solution from our Colonel that should make everyone happy. Let us divide the land. Most of Rockford is to the east of us and that is your land. We'll move west, towards Milwaukee."

"That section right there is in Rockford. I want it moved at least fifty miles from our border," The man with the biggest gun countered.

"We'll move that part of the wall north-west, as long as you promise no violence. I need a guarantee you won't use those guns on our people once my back is turned. One bullet and all bets are off," Antonio said sternly, hoping they'd agree.

"I ain't aiming to kill any man and don't want to start a war. We carry guns to protect our family. There's a few more of us and we've got a good set up here. Go your way and let us live our way undisturbed." The man with the gun in Blake's face took a step back after he spoke. It appeared the gun-toting gang had no desire to escalate the matter further. Antonio had to trust things were as they appeared.

"Fair deal. Now, these formidable individuals will remain here to act as a blockade for my troops while we start moving these poles out of Rockford. I'd appreciate it if you stop pointing your guns at these fine human beings for the remainder of this process, so we ensure there are no nasty incidents," Antonio continued firmly negotiating his terms for their informal truce.

"Stand down. Slowly," The man commanded his pose while lowering his own magnum. The remaining seven gunmen followed suit.

"Thank you, sincerely. We will be out of your way as quickly as possible." Antonio waved towards her team. They used the backhoe to dig out and hoist the poles back onto the flatbeds. The team pulled up every foot of wall until they reached the outskirts of town. They switched directions and began repositioning them west of their original route, but still traveling around Great Lakes north back into Canada.

Antonio was impressed they were able to quickly calm the would-be robbers and called to thank her once they had built enough wall to report their mission was no longer in duress, "It worked, Colonel. We lost a bit of Illinois, but we're still able to surround the Lakes. Most importantly, no one got hurt."

"I appreciate you handling such a delicate situation on our behalf. I will support any solution you implement in my absence as long as it doesn't go against the principles of B.E.ST. If we can't solve it peacefully, then I would like to be involved." Amica couldn't be everywhere and trusted her team had the good judgment to lead without her guidance.

"Thank you for your trust. I have a few team members scouting a spot to rest for the evening and will report back tomorrow on our progress. Have a good night, Colonel," Antonio replied sincerely.

Once reassured that the frontline troops were safe, Amica checked in with Arturo on their online foe. "Any new DMs from Mr. Big Gun or his bot friends?"

"Yes, but it was the identical wording with the same follow-up message," Her assistant answered.

"We can't let one person deter us. Monitor the situation closely and advise me immediately if anything changes," The Colonel commanded firmly.

"Will do, Colonel Harrison!" Arturo responded with a salute.

"Thank you. Please enjoy your evening and we will reconnect in the morning." A simple nod from Amica was given before both retired for the night. Colonel Harrison felt reassured that her second encounter with gun slingers ended even better than her first. It was the boost of confidence she needed.

Fort Wayne Family

It took three and half weeks for the team to finish the American side of the wall, which was considerably faster than the Colonel had estimated. The only other outsiders they encountered *en route* was a blended family of seven who had commandeered a ski resort. Thankfully the group was welcoming almost immediately and were sincerely interested in joining B.E.S.T. The family signed the contract without hesitation and then made enough pasta with butter and cheese to feed the entire crew.

The southern portion of the wall project was wrapped up mid-August, but it still wasn't enough to keep everyone safe. The builders left a few people behind every few miles to guard the interior perimeter during construction. Those team members could claim that zone as their future home or come back to the Trenton base once things settled down on the former American side.

Six people who had all known each other previously made the choice to remain stateside after the southern section of the wall was complete. They discovered a spot with two corn fields, a pear tree, wild asparagus, and an old store that still hadn't been looted for canned goods. The Colonel agreed to send them a POP for transportation, plus plants and seeds to start their own southern colony.

The B.E.S.T. team in Fort Wayne, Indiana consisted of a mother named Melanie, her daughter Rose, and Rose's boyfriend Matt, as well as their closest friends, Shara and Dodi, and the house's handyman, Xavier.

The happy group scouted out a fifty- and a forty-acre estate within a few miles of the border. Rose and Matt took over the smaller mansion on the hill, whereas the friendly foursome chose a Victorian-style fortress with its own private lake. Within days, they redecorated their new homes in their more colorful style and enthusiastically celebrated their involvement in rebuilding a new world.

"Never in my wildest dreams did I think I'd be laying down in a bed this big," Melanie exclaimed as she fell backwards onto the extended king in the master suite. The house had eighteen bedrooms in total and just the room itself was far bigger than her childhood home.

"Every bed in here is just as big. We could all claim two bedrooms for ourselves and there would still be room to spare," Dodi grinned.

"I want one on each side of the house, so I don't need to walk too far when I'm ready to crash!" Xavier suggestively smirked while slowly ripping off his shirt. His dark caramel skin was glistening from sweat. The group spent hours scouring their area on foot in the mid-summer humidity; all of them were drenched with sweat.

"The only thing I want is sleep," Melanie quickly quipped.

"Me too. Can we share that bed for now? Until I pick out my own? My legs hurt," Shara asked.

Melanie patted the spot next to her with a sad pout. "Okay, some snuggles, then sleep."

Shara dove into bed next to Melanie and they curled into each other. It was the most secure either woman had felt in years. They were next-door neighbors in Tecumseh, Ontario prior to joining B.E.S.T. Both worked in the hospitality industry and struggled financially after the world's third pandemic of the decade shut down their livelihoods yet again, this time without any government assistance.

Melanie moved in with Shara first, then Melanie's daughter Rose joined with Matt, soon followed by Dodi, and eventually Xavier moved into the basement. Xavier had been a cook who suddenly found himself homeless after his restaurant closed. Unwilling to let him suffer sleeping on the streets, they offered the somewhat-better concrete basement floor. The group fought for every cent and scraped by just to survive, as did most people in the late 2030's.

Blended family homes became more common as resources began to diminish, threats of violence became more prominent, and the cost of living far exceeded the average income. Now, suddenly, the same six people were living in exquisite mansions with an army of support. Since there were no other people around, they roamed the city wild and free, blasting music and dancing in the streets.

On the fourth day after the wall was complete, the Colonel sent POPs to the team members who chose to stay on the American side. This would make it easier for them to travel back and forth to the base when needed.

Unfortunately, not one of the six had any experience flying. They could never afford a POP; they barely had enough to buy nutritional supplements. Thankfully, the teammate who dropped off the mini plane gave a basic explanation of how it worked, which seemed simple enough.

Matt and Rose were the first to take it for a ride, hovering only a few feet above the ground until they got used to manipulating the controls. Melanie tugged and twirled her thick golden braid obsessively while watching the small plane above her. The young couple took turns flying and would switch places in the cabin each time they waited for the panels to be recharged. They eagerly volunteered to be the Fort Wayne flyers for their family, scouting for food sources and potential threats.

"Mom, you should try it. It is so cool weaving back and forth between buildings. Way more fun than driving, but you'll still feel safe!" Rose couldn't help herself from talking a mile a minute after their first long flight around Indiana. Mimicking her mother's habit, she twisted her long blonde strands around her finger as spoke.

"No, thanks. I like my feet on the ground," Melanie said while shaking her head.

"Your feet wouldn't be so sore from walking everywhere if you learn to fly," Rose argued back.

"I love walking. It keeps my body in shape. Maybe one day I'll let you fly me around, but not today, kid." Melanie gave her petite daughter a big squeeze and quickly changed the conversation before Rose could talk her into a ride in the POP. "Let's go jump in the lake instead."

Melanie wasn't the adventurous type until her little girl grew up to be fearless. Rose had convinced her to go on a roller coaster, attend a concert in Detroit, and ride on the back of her motorcycle. Every moment of each experience terrified Melanie, but she couldn't say no to her favorite girl.

"Fine, but you will fly one day. I will make sure of it," Rose insisted.

The mother-daughter duo took off running and were quickly joined by the other four. The six new residents of Fort Wayne spent the rest of the day soaking in their new surroundings on the lake with a fabulous feast and a couple bottles of vintage wine they found in the mansion's cellar.

Life had never been better.

Jammed with Spam

The misinformation campaign was finally progressing and they had almost filled one ship to Australia. Financially, they could afford the expensive fuel now that they received the massive payment in full from two hundred and sixty-three excited passengers. Since the campaign hadn't attracted as many people as she hoped, the Colonel decided to reduce it from three vessels to one, making it significantly easier to supply adequate security.

After fuel, food supply for the passengers, and a budget for a lavish welcome home party for the crew in anticipation of a successful mission, they had over thirty-two million dollars to spare. Money was a rare and highly sought-after commodity that still could be used in the bartering of anything from anyone. Large amounts were kept electronically in secure holdings by one of the few legitimate banks still in existence.

Thanks to Kristie's connections, Leamington was blooming into a thriving group of grow houses and corn fields providing essentials to the B.E.S.T. community. Two million was given to the municipality of Leamington and another one million each to the four most productive grow houses. This influx in cash was provided in exchange for producing enough tomatoes, cucumbers, green beans, peppers, corn, and cannabis to supply every B.E.S.T. team member.

The Colonel allocated two million to Forest Ranger Robert to source and transport seedlings from British Columbia and Alberta, and the forests between Washington State and Montana, to Algonquin Park. She posted a one million dollar investment opportunity to anyone who had a solution that would make B.E.S.T. even better, and then tucked the rest away in a secured online currency account to stimulate the economy later on.

As a result of their efforts, they recruited thousands of new members who traveled from all over Canada and the Northern State Community to sign up, even a few who were genuine New United Republic converts that realized violence hadn't served them well. Several leaders from other small countries and the remaining Asian Naturalists, whom Commander Ying recruited, all gathered their resources and moved into their new utopia. People and food were pouring in from all sides.

Everything appeared to be going according to plan.

As life had taught Amica over and over again, smooth sailing can change into a violent storm without warning. Just as they were finalizing the guest and cargo list for the trip to Australia, the recruitment account became flooded with death threats. The wall they built was no longer a secret in the South and members of N.U.R. were furious to discover they were being cut off from the Great Lakes and vast resources within Canada.

The southern half of North America was an undeniable shitshow, literally sinking by the day. Many of the rebels were already planning to overthrow Canadians and steal their resources long before the campaign went into effect. Once they found out there was honest hope of replenishing the earth's natural supply, they wanted to claim their share.

Unfortunately, they weren't willing to work for it.

Caravans full of N.U.R. leaders were migrating north to see what would be necessary to take down the wall. The southern shoreline was shrinking, and deadly tropical storms had destroyed more of the coast through the summer months. They originally congregated in the southern states due to their appreciation for a warmer climate, but the harsh winters were no longer the greater threat to their survival.

N.U.R. was run by a cast of entitled elitists, or violent robbers who either inherited their wealth and power, or stole it from someone who did. The eldest two sons of impeached President Trump each took a short turn trying to control the unruly population before relinquishing all power and hiding from the mob. Trump's sons were now using their vast wealth to pay security and support staff to maintain a safe and luxurious lifestyle for their families, isolated deep within the mountains of northern Texas.

There was no longer any organized leadership. Money and violence ruled. You either bribed, threatened, fought, or shot your way out of every situation. Although the New United Republic consisted of well over a million people, all of the country's money belonged to only a few thousand people, most of whom jumped at a chance to buy a better life in Australia.

The majority of its people were poor, fighting daily to survive. Some would run errands for the wealthy in exchange for food. Others would scavenge abandoned stores or use makeshift weapons to rob another who happened to be more fortunate than themselves. The Colonel's plan sent N.U.R. reeling into bedlam.

Dixon, River, Junior, and Alora survived by living in the shadows and watching each other's backs. They saw both campaigns, scanned the article headlines, and were weighing their choices on a humid afternoon in August.

"We need to find a way to smuggle ourselves on that ship," Dixon argued.

"Do you know how far it is to Australia? You can't hide on a boat for the entire time," Alora fired back, followed by a frustrated sigh.

"What we need is to get the cash on the ship ASAP. Isn't there still that old celebrity couple in Georgia with the pathetic security detail?" Junior joined the discussion. "I know we didn't want to drive that far south, but isn't that where the ship is sailing from anyway?"

"I heard a gang from the Georgia prison got to them first," Dixon replied.

"What about joining the other side?" Alora thought out loud. "It sounds like they will supply food and shelter in exchange for pitching in our share of the workload. Would that be so bad?"

"No weapons allowed? That's the problem," River piped up. "They want a gun-free zone, which is suspicious to me. Someone there will have a gun and will make everyone else their slave in no time."

The foursome sat silently, staring at the motionless world surrounding them. They were currently holding out in a boarded-up bowling alley in Columbus, Ohio. It had a freezer full of frozen fried crap when they first took it over, and they had consumed enough onion rings and french fries to pad their skinny frame. Their bodies desperately needed fresh vegetation and exercise to balance the pounds of saturated fats.

"Wait a second, folks. If the people building this better world up north don't have weapons or believe in violence, they're easy targets." A smile took over Dixon's face. "We can be that someone with a gun!"

"We don't have a gun, dude," River interjected.

"We have firecrackers, a flare gun, a taser, a shit load of knives, and several grenades," Dixon countered. "It's enough to intimidate them into compliance. We don't even need to hurt someone to prove our dominance."

"We can send them threatening DMs from a bunch of different fake accounts while we're *en route* so they're already on edge when we get there. They don't need to know there are only four of us." Alora was already mentally packing their limited belongings.

"We have enough fireworks to loudly announce our arrival. Then we toss one grenade into their troops to show we're serious and use the others as leverage to ensure they obey." River smirked.

"We don't need to set off a grenade; we just need to scare them. This plan might work." Junior nodded in agreement.

"The new world they're building needs leaders who aren't afraid to flex their muscles. They need protection. We're going to show them that they need us." Dixon sounded as confident as he felt.

"I think you're right, Dix. We'll never rule with the wealthy in Australia, but we can with the unarmed up North," Alora added.

"So, we're really going north?" River asked.

"Yep!" Dixon responded without hesitation.

"Guess I should layer up on these bowling shirts," River replied.

"Probably should grab a couple jackets for each of us, too. It will be cold." Dixon started scanning the place for anything that might be of use. "I bet we could use bowling pins as clubs if anyone steps out of line."

"What about bowling balls?" River asked with the utmost sincerity.

"Really?" Alora replied with a snort.

"We will need to carry everything in our backpacks. How strong do you think you are?" Junior flexed his own impressive muscles, taunting the slim, shorter man standing in front of him.

"Ten-pound ball wouldn't be a problem for me." River grabbed a black and purple swirl-patterned ball from the rack next to him. He pumped the ball in the air with one arm, pressing it like a dumbbell, to show off his lean, yet solid forearms.

"Put the ball down and focus. We have a long way to go and need to travel intelligently." Dixon's stare forced the ball from River's hand back into the rack. Although there had never been a set leader, the team knew not to mess with Dixon. They witnessed him slit a woman's throat in Georgia because she wouldn't take off her diamond necklace. He didn't blink or hesitate as he pulled on the jewels tangled within her bloody hair. The foursome used the bowling alley for one final rest before heading north-east at sunrise.

Dixon and his friends' first stop was an old Ohio State University Airport. Two older pilots ran the abandoned airport, which consisted of only three planes. They had a four-seater that cost twelve thousand dollars per hour and two bigger planes that ran for nineteen and a half thousand dollars per hour, with a two hundred and fifty dollars per person seat charge.

"Unfortunately, we don't have the money for the fare, but we need to get into Canada. If you don't want us to make any trouble, I suggest you offer us a free lift." Dixon rested his right hand on his belt, showing where his long combat blade was secured in its holster.

"Everyone pays. We get threatened all the time and I don't give a flying fuck if you kill me. We're just hanging here waiting to die." Rank spittle flew at Dixon with each word.

"We have weapons and could steal everything you own. All we want is a flight into Canada," Dixon continued.

"And I've got a gun." The old man pulled a shiny black glock from inside his jacket.

"I suggest you four li'l' turds turn around if you don't want us to make any trouble," The other pilot chimed in.

The young gang retreated backwards, stopping only briefly to grab a bunch of green apples off a tree one block away. They found cars without gas, bicycles with flat tires, and no one willing to offer them a lift. It took nine days on foot, pillaging along the way, before they could see the new border.

"What the fuck is that?" Alora called out when the tall, plastic poles sticking out of large truck tires entered their line of sight.

Fire in the Sky

It took a little more than a week for Rose to convince her mother Melanie to go for a spin in the POP. They were blissfully unaware of the threatening emails back at base camp and were frolicking gleefully around the streets of Fort Wayne, feeling like the war was won. They had ample housing, a fresh food supply, and the people who mattered most.

It was a clear day; the sun illuminated every corner of the sky and their POP had a full charge. Shara, Dodi, and Melanie spent the morning swimming and were lounging on three oversized plush ottomans in the master dressing room.

Rose and Matt spent their morning touring in the POP, looking for supplies and any living creatures. They had already covered everything within a fifteen-mile radius and were running out of places to loot.

Although the building team gathered what they could from each area as they built the wall, there was the potential for more food sources a few miles south.Rose was worried that angry southerners had gathered on the other side and were planning a strike. Some nights she was convinced she heard shouting bouncing around in the air. She wanted to know if they were really safe. Unfortunately Matt disagreed and wouldn't go with her, insisting they were safer following the Colonel's orders

"You don't want me to peer over the wall on my own, so come with me. I'm going to try today with or without you. Someone should come along for the ride or else I might end up in the Caribbean, floating away on a sinking island," Rose teased, waving a snack bag filled with veggies and their homemade hummus in front of her mom. "I even prepared a mid-flight meal."

"You make it impossible to say no," Melanie replied with a wide smile.

"Let's move it before you change your mind," Rose exclaimed. She gave Matt a quick kiss goodbye, grabbed her mom's hand, and started pulling her towards the small plane.

"Fine, but just over the wall enough to see if there's any sign of life. We're not landing on the other side." She pulled her thick blonde curls back into a scrunchie as she answered, ready for their next adventure..

"Deal! Now hop to it," Rose enthusiastically replied.

The giddy pair boarded the egg-shaped craft, buckled up, and Rose flicked a switch, turning the motor on. "You'll feel a little jolt when we take off. It's normal. The wings start out like a helicopter when it lifts off, then transition horizontally before we go forward. The plane will drop slightly during the transition, but it's literally a two second, few-inch drop. You've got this, Mom."

Melanie's eyes squeezed tighter together with each word. Rose waited until they were inside the POP to give her mom the scary details; a warning was necessary to avoid a freak out. Her mom loved adventure, however she needed a little help getting the first foot out the door.

Rose kept the plane only a few feet above the ground, waiting for her mom to reopen her eyes. Within a few short minutes, Melanie slowly spread her eyelids apart and absorbed the new infinite view. A loud sigh was followed instantly with an enthusiastic smile.

"Do you like it? I'm going to go a little faster and higher if you're ready," Rose asked, slowly accelerating while rising on a twenty-degree incline.

"Do what you got to do, girl. This is good." Melanie's back was still pressed firmly against the back of her chair, but her breathing had returned to normal. She admired her daughter's courage, motivating her to dig deep enough to find her own.

It was a smooth ride up to twelve feet when they began approaching the wall. The top of the poles were a few feet higher than their current elevation. Rose pulled back, attempting to rise high enough to fly over.

Their speed dropped instead of accelerating as expected. The POP started to vibrate, and both ladies trembled while a warning flashed in vibrant red across the dash, "DO NOT EXCEED TWELVE FEET. STOP. *ARRÊT.* HALT. *PARAR,*" echoed in the small chamber.

"Stop, Rose. I don't think a POP can fly that high. Go down, Rose, please," Melanie insisted frantically, and Rose descended without argument.

"Sorry, Mom, I didn't mean to scare you." Rose apologized sincerely, hiding her disappointment.

"I'm okay. It was awesome being in the air that high. I'd go again, just don't exceed ten feet," Melanie replied.

"The POP can go up to twelve feet, Mom," Rose explained.

"You can go up to ten feet, especially if I'm in the POP," Melanie clarified with a stern look and a soft motherly smile.

"I bet the wall was deliberately built high enough that you can't get a POP over it. The Colonel created quite the clever plan," Rose pondered out loud.

After they returned at their new home, it occurred to Rose that the wall was created not only to keep anyone from coming in, but to ensure no one could get out. "How will we know if a threat is approaching if we can't look over the wall?"

"What about a drone? I found one in the shed when you ladies were gone," Matt chimed in as he greeted them in the driveway. "It needs batteries. I bet one of these places has some stuff in a drawer."

"Brilliant idea! There are enough bedrooms in this house, someone must have batteries in their nightstand." Rose gave him a high-five before taking off in search of some lithium batteries to test their new toy.

"I think we need to extend the moat we dug during the build. We'll widen the trench and fill it with the more dangerous creatures we pull from the lakes around here," Shara added.

"What, frogs and fish?" Dodi questioned.

"More like the sea lamprey and snakehead fish I saw when we were fishing," Matt advised.

"Those were nasty," Rose confirmed.

"Smarter to assume we'll eventually be under attack and prepare rather than get caught off guard." Melanie shared her daughter's doubts that their perfect new world would remain untouched.

The Fort Wayne team was ready to take action. They found batteries for the drone and flew it over the wall first thing the following morning. Rose was nervous that she'd lose the drone or attract attention if she went too far, and ended up not going far enough to actually see anyone. They felt somewhat reassured that no one was standing directly on the other side working towards making their way over.

Matt and Rose's new home was within a mile of the southernmost tip of the wall, and the foursome of friends lived only a couple more miles further north. To protect their property, they marched one hundred feet in front of their front door and dug a three-foot-wide ditch surrounding the southern side of their land.

There was already a narrow ditch alongside the recycled border wall, created through the construction process of planting the poles. They took ten wide steps from the edge of the construction trench and started digging a four-foot-wide hole, using the dirt they pulled out to build a wall on the northern side.

Their old-school-style security system had a deep drop if you jumped directly off of the wall, a small, almost-barren patch of land, then a large pit, eventually to be filled with water and slimy creatures, followed by half a mile of abandoned homes, before encountering their second ditch surrounding the closest house to the border.

"A moat and the ditch provides a little added protection. Now we can return to enjoying life! We've worked hard our whole lives. It's time for us to reap the rewards without stressing over what might happen," Matt proclaimed proudly.

"Three cheers to that!" Dodi lifted her glass of vintage wine that they rescued from the basement cellar to toast the completion of the first one thousand feet of trench.

It took over a week, working only for a few hours early each morning to avoid the humidity and crisp scorch of summer sun. They swam in the afternoon, drank in the early evening, and climbed into bed as soon as the sun went down.

"I'd join the celebration, but my shoulders are too sore to lift the glass." Melanie was stretched out on a plush chaise lounger with her eyes closed.

"When we searched the pharmacy's stockroom up the road, we were only looking for food and vitamins. We'll go back tonight and see if they have anything for your back pain," Rose offered immediately.

"A heating pack or heat rub would be perfect. I wonder if it closed up shop before codeine was banned. Grab any painkillers you find, just in case," Melanie answered.

"Got it, Mom. I'll just take anything I think we might need, including First Aid supplies. I cut my leg and had to fashion a bandaid out of toilet paper. Luckily that's the one thing all these old houses are stocked up on. Remember the house with cases of toilet paper in the basement?" Rose turned to Matt, shaking her head in disbelief.

"People thought the world was going to run out of trees, and that's not too far off. Be grateful you have something to wipe your ass with," Xavier tossed his two cents in.

"Super grateful!" Rose fired back. She meant it. Her mother always made sure that she had everything she needed, though they still struggled and made sacrifices. They were now in their own protected community with everything they needed and everyone they loved.

The pair took a forty-five-minute power nap after their dinner of freshly-picked corn, grilled peppers, and oat cakes with mashed apples. Matt put on the kettle and made two black teas in to-go cups, while Rose gathered a few reusable bags and a knife for protection. So far they hadn't encountered anyone with ill intentions, but it was still a possibility. Their location was a little too south for her liking.

They intentionally took streets they hadn't walked down prior, looking for places that could house more supplies. Their pantry was currently stocked with canned vegetables and soups, fruit spreads, Quaker oats, and wine. They were able to collect fresh fruits and vegetables, but no potatoes, or more importantly, potato chips.

"Remember Ruffles with Heluva Good dip? I'd give anything for a real potato chip," Matt commented after exiting another convenience store that only had cat food and paper towels left on its shelves.

"Mmm...Dill Pickle! It feels like forever." Rose bit her lower lip instinctually, reminiscing of her old favorite.

"Rose, get back here now," A voice echoed eerily through the empty streets.

"Is that my mom?" Rose asked Matt, looking in the direction of the home.

"We're under attack." This time the words were rising from a shadow, rounding a corner over a block away.

"Under attack?" Matt shouted back as he and Rose searched the streets for signs of a looming threat

"Where are they, Mom?" Rose called out.

"Look up. Up above," Melanie called out into the sky just as it burst into violent embers.

The sky was on fire.

99

The Impenetrable Wall

The four vagabonds from Ohio arrived at the new border midday and decided to rest for a moment to discuss how they could strike fear on the other side. They increased the number of email threats *en route*, but had yet to receive a response.

"We can get on top of the tires, but the poles are too close together. We can't wiggle through them." Alora had pulled herself up high enough to see on top of the tire stacks, however the poles prevented her from seeing any further. She tried to pull herself all the way up, but the poles were too slippery to get a proper grip.

"If we get the right tools, we could cut through the poles," River suggested.

"There are a lot of poles and they're thick," Alora fired back.

"A two-inch PVC pipe cutter will do the trick," River replied.

"They felt solid and over three inches thick," Alora argued.

Dixon walked over to where Alora was standing at the base of the wall. He tried to wedge his feet between the tires the way Alora did, to hoist himself higher enough to reach the poles, but his feet wouldn't fit.

"Junior, River, come on, help boost me up there. I need to see exactly how it's built," Dixon called and both men came running. They each took a foot, while he gripped onto the tires, then the poles. His hands slid along the slick poles and he scrambled to pull himself high enough to get a good view. There were too many poles in front of him to count.

"She's right. The poles felt solid and very slippery. We're going to need a reciprocating saw, plus a ladder to get all the way on top," Dixon confirmed. "We'll rest for a bit, have an apple and some water before looking for a hardware store."

The team took a twenty-minute nap on the grass and woke up refreshed and eager to tackle the next challenge. They had slept fairly well in a filthy hotel the night prior and were used to wandering all day on foot.

"Junior, River, and I will go on the hunt for the right tools. Alora will stay here and guard our belongings. While we're gone, I need you to escalate the threat. Say that we're going to start firing grenades over the wall if they don't grant us access in the next twenty-four hours.

There has to be an opening somewhere. Send them DMs from every account we have set up, and if you have time, set up more," Dixon directed his loyal follower and occasional lover.

"Would we even be able to toss a grenade over that wall? It's fucking high, and pretty wide. Maybe we should threaten to use them to blow up the wall," Alora suggested.

"That's a bad idea, 'cause they'll be waiting on the other side with whatever they can fashion into weapons. We need to say random bombs over the wall, so the Colonel knows her people are in danger," Dixon insisted.

"But if the Colonel knows the bombs won't make it over the wall, then she'll know this is a hollow threat." Alora was used to holding her ground with these three persistent men.

"Do you have a solution or are you just poking holes in every one of my plans?" Dixon inquired.

"What about a slingshot?" Junior asked.

"That could work. We could say we've built a slingshot to launch the grenades." Alora was grateful for Junior's support. Dixon was more a dictator than a debater.

"Fine. Go with that, just make it convincing," Dixon demanded before the three men ventured in search of tools.

Alora fired off the first email before the men were out of sight.

Colonel.

We are at your doorstep. It's an interesting wall you've created in Indiana. Interesting, but not impenetrable.

We're putting together massive slingshots to fire grenades over your border. If you don't grant us access through the wall within twenty-four hours, we're going to launch one grenade over it to show we are serious. We will continue to launch random grenades over the wall until you let us in.

Our army awaits your response.

Sincerely, Your Commander.

Similar versions of the same message began flooding their recruitment account and Colonel Harrison couldn't ignore it. Her technical advisor felt certain the messages were coming from one central location, even though there were now over several dozen profiles uttering similar threats.

"Please send communication to all the locations along the border that they are to move a minimum of two miles from the border and to advise immediately if they see any flash of light. You can inform them that a threat has been made and we are verifying its credibility. Make sure to notify the group in Fort Wayne along the Indiana border first," The Colonel instructed Arturo.

"Of course. Is there anything else I can do to help?" Arturo asked..

"Actually, there is. I have a tough decision to make. Can you ask a few people to meet me in my office? Come back when you're done sending the warning. I'd like your opinion as well." The Colonel wasn't sure how to handle the threat and wanted more perspectives before making her next move.

"Yes, Colonel. I'll do whatever I can to protect our people. It shouldn't take me long at all to send the messages," Arturo answered.

"Please use direct voice messaging and a wrist alert. They have a right to know as soon as possible," Amica added.

"Will do!" Arturo gave a quick salute before hustling to his desk to start sending alerts.

It was too soon for Amica to waiver on her no-violence-allowed policy, but she would need an effective response if they followed through on the grenade threat. Protecting her people was the first priority, however, and if they didn't respond, future attacks would escalate. The Colonel knew to avoid an all-out war at all costs.

Catastrophic Confidence

While Amica was carefully evaluating her next move, a wicked storm was brewing south of the border. The three mischievous men boisterously returned from their scouting trip, hands full of supplies. They even scored three big bags of peanuts, a treat they hadn't seen in months. Chins up, feeling invincible, they were ready for war.

The men did not find a suitable cutting tool for the poles, but had everything they needed to make a grenade slingshot and even found more explosives. Dixon was whipping his new rubber band from side to side as he approached Alora waiting by the wall.

"Ready to test our new toy?" He called out while snapping it in the air.

"We're not actually going to send a grenade?" Alora meant it as a statement, but her hesitation made it sound more like a question.

"Hell yeah! They need to know we're serious. We found more explosives at an old demolition company, including C-4 and military grade dynamite. Someone took all their tools, but left the best stuff behind." Dixon gave a frightening full-tooth grin precisely as thunder crackled in the distance.

"I thought the plan was to scare them?" Alora continued pushing.

"I'm tossing a grenade tonight, so they know that our threats weren't bullshit. We need to find a way in and I'm ready to knock so loud they can't ignore us." Dixon gave her a long, daring-her-to-argue stare.

He paced the area, looking for two trees strong enough and close together enough to hold the thick v-belt. Once Dixon selected the right trees, he used rope to secure an end of his homemade slingshot around the trunk of each tree. The other three watched without objection.

"Get some good-sized rocks and test it first. Maybe that will be enough to scare them and we won't need to send the grenade," Junior suggested in response to the worry resonating from Alora's face. Although they were accustomed to violence, starting a war might backfire.

There wasn't anything of the right shape in sight, so they ventured down the street until they found an old driveway that was crumbling. They gathered several baseball-sized chunks of broken cement and headed back to the wall. A few sprinkles of rain from the darkening clouds above scattered around them.

"Let's fire up this bad boy!" Dixon was jumping up and down like a kid on Christmas morning.

He pulled the band back tight, pulling it down and back to angle it towards the sky. His foot slipped once it was taut, causing him to launch it unexpectedly. The first test failed miserably, as the cement boulder shattered into pieces when it hit the low half of a pole.

"Fucking slippery mud." Dixon kicked the barely moist ground as River and Junior muffled their giggles. Alora stifled hers completely out of fear. She had seen his temper and didn't want to incite another incident.

He pulled it back again, cautious with his footing, and held it tight for a few seconds before sending flying through the air. It cleared the first pole, but a loud thud echoed back when it smacked into something along the way.

"That was close enough. Let's send the Colonel another threat first before launching one over," Alora insisted.

"They wouldn't hear that unless they're camped out directly on the other side. We need our first strike to make a real impact so they take us seriously." Dixon's eyes were focused on the funny-looking wall as he spoke.

Without hesitation he pulled the sling back as far as it could possibly stretch and slowly inched it lower than his previous shot, the band resisting every pull. Instead of scooping another boulder from his feet, he pulled the grenade out of the pocket in his cargo shorts. He looped his finger around the pin before resting it in the nook of the nylon slingshot.

"Bombs away, bitches!" Dixon screamed into the air as his finger slid out of the loop and the perfect pear-sized weapon soared high above the wall. Alora's mouth fell open; River's eyes doubled in size. Seconds felt like minutes before a blast consumed the sky.

"Again!" River shouted. "Aim some of those fireworks over the wall!"

"Patience. We have some beef jerky, baked beans, and peanuts that I want first. We'll take a nap, refuel, and if they haven't responded in the next hour, then the fireworks begin," Dixon decided for everyone.

He paced the ground, weighing the various outcomes as his team divided up the snacks. No injuries or minimal damage meant he would have to waste more of his limited weaponry. Destruction or loss of human life could inspire violent retaliation from the peacekeepers. Dixon was secretly hoping to merely scare a few and shatter enough of the wall to break though.

Way Too Fast

When The Colonel called to warn the Fort Wayne team of a grenade threat, Melanie didn't stop long enough to catch her breath or consider sending the Colonel or her daughter an urgent connect alert in return. Instead, she shoved her feet into her worn out runners, sans socks, and yelled to the group, "Be right back. I'm going to tell Rose and Matt to come home now."

Melanie was an avid walker, but the full-out run she attempted amped up her usual pace. Her lungs forced her to slow down just in time to avoid the trench surrounding the property. She saw two figures several streets ahead and tried calling out to them. They couldn't hear her, so she walked around to a storage shed on this side of the pit, where they kept a thick board to make it easier to cross.

The board was heavy and awkward to balance with just one person. Never one to back down from a challenge or ask for help, she teetered it back and forth, smacking herself both in the forehead and shin as she went. The fear of her daughter being exposed to a grenade blast because she was taking such good care of her mom,like always, pushed her until she was on the other side. Lightening brightened the sky beyond the wall, propelling Melanie's feet even faster.

Melanie called out again as loud as she could and this time heard a faint sound in response. She could also see bright red and orange stars heading in her direction. She screamed, "Look up, up above" into the night sky, and poof, it was over. The impact sent her backwards into the moat, where the ashes and embers from the explosion laid her to rest.

Black smoke consumed the charcoal sky.

After minutes of shocked silence, Matt called Shara to confirm that her, Dodi, and Xavier were safe inside and were filled in on the warning from the Colonel. Shara asked if Melanie had reached them in time and Matt sank to the ground, knowing what he feared was true.

Rose knew the figure before them had been her mother. She was paralyzed, staring into the wall of fire in front of her. She saw exactly what happened, but it happened so fast that it couldn't possibly have happened. It was way too fast to be real.

Amica's hands trembled as Matt relayed the tragic news to her. She offered her condolences and promised help was on the way. Her stomach sank, and her body followed as she sank onto the floor beneath her. It wasn't the first casualty on her watch, and every life lost still haunted her. This one stung especially hard considering it happened in a war she had inadvertently created.

The safety measures she took were not enough; she wasn't willing to risk more lives in the process. Debates on their next move had already begun and were still in progress when the Colonel received Matt's call. Several entertaining and plausible suggestions had been made, most of which would require a little more planning, or bordered on violence. They weren't expecting a battle to break out this quickly.

The clock hadn't run out; Melanie's clock shouldn't have run out.

"The horrific news we just received requires a faster response. They didn't allow us the time they promised, and we must act swiftly before more lives are lost. For now, I've asked the team in Fort Wayne, Indiana to move as far away from the wall as possible. I'm assuming they don't have full-sized planes, otherwise they wouldn't have launched the grenade from the other side."

"We can get a few crop dusters from Leamington and there's two working fighter jets back at the base. Going with tonight's non-lethal suggestions, we will do three drops, two planes per drop. Load one will be the sap and maple syrup, then dried pine needles and seagull feathers, followed by all those corn husks from our last cookout." The Colonel's face was dead serious, for she knew their bombs seemed somewhat trivial.

"Captain John, Tamika, and Bryan will drive the prisoners down to Tallahassee for the ship destined for Australia. Josée, you'll coordinate the drops and be the eye in the sky for this mission, then meet up with the ship before it departs. Kali, Chris, Carter, Tobin, and Pynk will be the other five pilots. I'm going to visit the teams along the border to show our commitment to them, starting with Fort Wayne.

"Once all loads have been deployed on the targets, I need everyone to return the planes back to the base immediately, except Josée. Rose deserves better border security and you're the best I know. Meet me at their new home; it's a golf course in Auburn, Indiana about a hundred miles north of our wall. Does everyone understand the plan?" The Colonel spoke as quickly and clearly as she could.

"Yes, Colonel" sounded off from the special project recruits, except Josée. She waited for the enthusiastic responses to die down before interjecting.

"I get the annoyance of the bomb you're dropping, but these are murderers. They killed one of us. Sticky shit and corn cobs aren't going to cut it. We need something with more force," Josée shouted at the Colonel passionately.

"The point is to show them we have multiple planes, followed by a threat that the next drop will be deadly. I'm not willing to risk more lives in a war," The Colonel calmly explained.

"War's inevitable, but I got ya, boss. We can discuss next steps once we land in Fort Wayne." Josée's lips pressed firmly together, teeth loudly grating on top of one another. She wanted war, but she'd wait to see what the Colonel had planned.

"Everyone gather as much as you can into the potato sacks by the barracks and meet me inside the hangar in thirty minutes." The Colonel pointed towards the piles of corn husks and pine cones that had been collected over the past few weeks. As her team headed towards them, she gently touched Josée's hand before she could take off. "Come with me for a moment, Josée; I'd like to chat a bit."

"I didn't mean to question your command in front of everyone. I'd rather eat maple syrup than waste it on murderers. Don't you think it's a mild response to an offensive murder?" Josée stated, clearly annoyed.

"I don't mind that you questioned my orders and I appreciate you speaking your mind. I need to hear diverse opinions when I'm making tough decisions. This is not a dictatorship, nor is it a violent society. Lethal force is always a last resort," Amica said, displaying a willingness to bend.

"I get your savvy strategies for dealing with troublemakers, but the consequence for intentionally causing death must be death." Josée stood firm, hands on her hips.

"If each death results in death, life will soon fail to exist. We want a world without war and it would be inevitable if we retaliate. Your way might be the only way that ends up working, but I'd rather try scaring them first. If it fails, I'll put you in charge of ensuring they don't strike back," The Colonel offered a compromise to show her respect for her colleague's perspective.

"In charge? Doesn't that mean I can handle it my way?" Josée's eyebrows raised higher with each word.

"Yes," Amica conceded.

"Alright. Let's start with the sticky dump shit and escalate if necessary. Do we know the location and size of the target?" Josée appreciated the Colonel's willingness to bend, and felt compelled to do the same.

"Rose flew a drone over and believes that they're only four people. The only other sign of life she saw within miles was an elderly couple tending to a garden. Neither of us feels they would have been involved." The Colonel grabbed a piece of paper from the folder she was holding and handed it to Josée. "Here are the new coordinates for the Fort Wayne team and here's where the four targets were last seen."

"Looks like at least a hundred miles in between. How secluded are they?" She asked while reviewing the directions and map, absorbing every detail.

"Rose said there are lots of trees surrounding the perimeter, and it's an unlikely home, so they feel protected. They're using the drone to make sure the wall hasn't been compromised. She's getting anxious and has prepared manure bombs to shoot over the wall with a Nerf water balloon launcher. Rose wants to send them from her POP, staying on our side of the wall. I agreed, as long as she's protected," Amica explained.

"Of course that won't be enough to discourage them, so I told her she could send them simultaneously as you overturn the barrels of sap on them. The attack has to happen quickly and then she needs to fly back home immediately. Keeping Rose safe is your first priority," The Colonel continued.

"I'm entrusting you, Josée, to make sure that happens." Amica placed both hands on Josée's shoulders while maintaining a few feet of distance. Physical closeness was frowned upon after the pandemics; any contact signified deep trust and connection.

"On my honor," Josée replied with a sincere salute.

"Thank you. I'll see you after the strike and we can evaluate our next move together." With that one last reassurance that the Colonel would do whatever needed to be done, the strike team was on their way.

It was smooth sailing on their way to the border, and the team was waiting in position for Matt to peek the drone far enough over the wall to reconfirm their target's position. He could see four beings resting under the shade of a large evergreen. They were using their backpacks as pillows, and had their more destructive supplies collected in a locked box up against the tree behind them. The sole key to the box was on a metal ring, secured to a chain around Dixon's sweat-covered neck.

Six planes flew over the wall, two by two. The first pair opened their hatches and a gooey combination of sap and syrup poured over the pine tree, barely grazing the four below. It was enough to bolt them upright when the bags of needles and feathers rained down on their slightly sticky heads.

Whack. Smack.

Two balloons of shit burst as they struck branches, leaking rancid feces on the stunned foursome. More bombs fell around them, several landing on Alora and River's backpacks; a few could be seen hanging from the wall posts on the southern side. As they stood to shake the mess from their clothing, hundreds of brittle corn husks bounced off their bodies. A sharp edge slashed the side of Dixon's face on impact, before landing vertically planted inches into the ground.

"What the fuck!" He screamed up towards the clouds. Dixon and his friends watched the planes quickly loop around, back over the wall in which they came.

"Was this the response to the grenade?" Junior pondered out loud.

"Pretty weak response. They think a couple cuts and bruises will stop us." A large drop of sap fell from the tree above, landing directly on the new gash in his cheek. Dixon winced; a chuckle slipped from Alora's lips.

"We got a wrist message alert too," Alora interjected. "It says the sticky bombs are only the beginning. If we don't move, the next load they drop will be lethal."

"What the fuck? I thought it was a violence-free society." Dixon paced back and forth, needles falling from his clothes with each step.

"There's literal shit on my backpack, I pulled a nasty pine needle out of my arm, and I've got a goose egg from a corn husk bomb. I'm done." River grabbed his bag, holding it an arm's length away from his chest, and started walking towards a river they encountered earlier in their travels.

"Wait, River, I'll join you," Alora called after him while gathering her belongings.

"Are you fucking kidding me!" Dixon screamed. "Fucking chicken shits, running over syrup and feathers. You 'fraid they gonna drop pancakes and applesauce next?"

"What if it's bricks or bowling balls, remember that idea? Might have been a dumb idea to carry them all this distance, but they could use the same weapon to kill us." Junior jumped to his feet, picked up his sack, shook off the pine needles and feathers, and raced to catch up with River and Alora.

"Weak! You're as weak as them!" Dixon sat on the box of weapons, which the other three had failed to remember. He whispered to himself, "And now I have all the power. Those pathetic hypocrites will pay for this!"

Hole Drilling 101

It was a blisteringly hot day and Ariel spent the morning harvesting vegetables with Royelle, Bella, Sarah, and Arturo. Lettuce, tomatoes, peppers, and green onions were popping up everywhere, which was ideal since they were running low on food. She was drenched from the sun's fierce rays and wanted nothing more than to stand underneath an ice cold shower.

Arturo's phone rang while they were walking side by side, each holding the handle of a large rattan basket full of produce. They stopped to put down the one hundred or so peppers they collected so he could retrieve the phone from the pocket in his khaki shorts.

"I understand. I'm sure we can come up with something. I'm with Ariel and Sarah now. I'll grab Dawna and Calvin as well." Arturo turned on his conversation recorder before repeating back to the Colonel, "Six hard rubber panels, thirty-six by six feet, with holes on a slant so they can be attached to our current wall. Got it."

Arturo hung up the phone and turned to Ariel. "The Colonel has an urgent project. We'll drop these in the kitchen and tell Sarah. I'll let the rest of the team know that we are switching tasks. Can you find Calvin and Dawna? I think they're in the old command center."

"You've got it!" Ariel shouted with a bit too much enthusiasm. She had been thinking about Calvin all morning, and was overly excited to see him.

Calvin was helping Dawna and Dr. Romano develop a small particle vacuum system for the hydro-filtration device they were using to clean the Great Lakes. After repeated use, small pieces were clogging the mesh, not allowing the water to filter through. The door was open, so she poked her head in.

"Dawna and Calvin? Arturo has an urgent task for us from the Colonel. Can you take a break from what you're working on?" Ariel spoke barely above a whisper, not looking directly at the group.

Doctor Ariel Sinclair had studied complex environmental health sciences through a University-level virtual program when she was only fifteen. At the age of eighteen, Ariel was the youngest doctor to be accredited through self-study examinations, and was qualified to practice both traditional and natural medicine in residential field hospitals. She was also the captain of her high school volleyball team and confident in her sleek physique. Her insecurities had never held her back.

Yet, somehow, with other strong women in the room, she felt an awkwardness around Calvin. He was attractive, successful, and smart, however those qualities were the furthest from her mind. His body made her weak and her animal instincts ruled, which might have explained why her words slipped out so quietly that the pair began walking towards her so they could hear Ariel better.

"Did you say an urgent task? Of course, if the Colonel needs us," Dawna replied eagerly.

Calvin lit up at the sight of her, as he visualized their prior spontaneous explosion of passion.

"Do you mind if we go, Gia? I'm sure Adam or Doctor Martin could help with the test model," Dawna asked her colleague.

"Go ahead. If Amica used the word urgent, it must be." Dr. Gia Romano waved them on their way.

The three scurried off to meet Arturo and Sarah. In less than fifteen minutes from when they arrived at the plant, they had prepared a sketch, a 3-D rendering, and a small-scale sample of the design. They hooked it onto the miniature wall prototype that was made months ago, and it worked. It only took the team another twenty minutes to replicate six more full-sized sheets.

Arturo arranged transportation while they were producing the final product. Within ninety-five minutes of the Colonel's phone call, they had her urgent request loaded on a trailer, headed to Fort Wayne, Indiana. Dawna was anxious to return to the vacuum trials with Doctor Romano, and Sarah announced that he was long overdue for a nap and a shower.

Calvin and Ariel enthusiastically volunteered to stay behind and clean the equipment. Ariel had been fantasizing about being with him since their last encounter and the way Calvin couldn't keep his eyes off of her, assured her that he felt the same. .

"We'll need to scrape off the melted rubber frame first, before sanitizing the table. What can we use that is hard and stiff?" Calvin suggestively asked.

"Hard and stiff? That shouldn't be too hard to find." Ariel blushed as moved closer to him.

Calvin leaned in for a kiss, which quickly led to grasping eagerly for every inch of each other. Being with one another intimately felt natural. The heat and passion was overwhelming, but there was something deeper burning between them. The wild groping session softly transitioned into a much longer embrace.

After what felt like minutes, Ariel pulled herself from him. "I guess we should get to work."

"Only if you promise I can kiss you again later." Calvin teased.

"I'm pretty sure that's a guarantee!" She responded while giving his butt a gentle tap.

Please Let Me Kill Him

After their unusual airstrike, Matt, Rose, and Josée took turns flying the drone to keep an eye on their reaction. They watched three of the four storm off and the fourth dude sulked on top of the box, possibly full of more grenades, or worse.

"He's planning his next move," Rose urged Josée and Amica.

"He hasn't done anything yet. It's only one man now," The Colonel attempted to reassure her.

"A dead man." Rose's stare burned through them before whipping herself around in a quick exit. She motioned for Matt who instinctually followed. They went outside to vent with Shara and Dodi.

"She wants blood and I'm willing to give her the peace she needs. You agreed we would try my way if yours didn't work," Josée reminded the Colonel after Rose exited through the large patio doors.

"Yes, but I have an idea that should still result in his ultimate demise, however I'd prefer if he was murdered by his own hands. I asked the team producing the wall pieces to develop a shield, which is being transported here as we speak. My plan is to erect it at the top of this side of the wall, so anything he throws over will bounce back his way," The Colonel quickly explained.

"That's brilliant!" Josée let a rare smile escape. "You should probably tell Rose before she goes off and does something herself."

"I was waiting to make sure it arrived before that clown tried anything else, otherwise I can't stop her from seeking revenge." Amica had a wrist alert tracking its arrival and knew it wouldn't be much longer.

Rose stormed into the former golf course's grand lobby, slamming the sliding glass door into its frame with enough force to smash the glass on impact. The loud bang snapped everyone to attention. Matt followed behind Rose unfazed, stepping over the tiny pieces scattered across the beige tile.

"He just set off fireworks inside the wall, chipping at the poles. Now he has a grenade in his hand. Please, let me kill him!" Rose's eyes were wide open and her first clenched tightly.

The Colonel recognized the anger and pain radiating through the genuinely sweet young woman. She had the same fiery rage in the middle of World War III. She was fighting both with and against Americans in Pittsburgh. It was during a brief moment in history where there were multiple enemies, including government and military personnel.

The reasons for the conflict varied from one coast to another. The east coast was shrinking, causing many to move inland, where property values rose well beyond what any middle class family could afford. Texas and other parts of the south closed their borders to all non-American-born citizens. The wicked race war escalated after the official division of the United States, and some Southerners were shooting anyone whose skin appeared darker than their own.

The main battlefield, said to decide the outcome of the United States of America, was taking place in Washington, D.C. It was a poorly-organized, endlessly-escalating violent chaos that had pedstrans battling the military with automatic weapons, families killing families, and no one willing to back down. It wasn't until the day every news station went black in protest of reading the daily obituaries that both sides agreed on a temporary ceasefire.

Two Senators, a Governor, a Mayor, three police officers, a first responder, an unarmed man, six armed men, a family of four, a baby, a grandfather, a doctor, two nurses, four high school students... All were tragically killed in D.C. on the same day. The unpredictable mass murders were becoming such a common occurrence that reporters couldn't cover all the significant members of their city who were gunned down in a fit of rage or simply killed over a clashing of opinions.

Europe was dealing with nuclear warfare in the Western hemisphere and didn't get into the Americans' civil madness. The Canadian government offered additional soldiers to protect the borders from the American side, as well as NAs, Northern Allies, who went undercover to divert attacks against the Capital. Before war officially broke out, Amica Harrison was asked to infiltrate the Trump family circle and warn of any deadly plans.

An American Military Officer with deep connections to Eric Trump and other affluent families beat and raped not only her, but two other associates. Amica couldn't say anything at the time without the risk of blowing her cover, plus he threatened that if she told anyone what he did, his friends could make her instantly disappear.

Private Harrison (her title at the time) received an intelligence briefing prior that gave her ample reasons to believe he could easily end her existence without consequence. Instead she insisted on being reassigned, suggesting her true identity had been exposed. She escaped in the middle of the night, unnoticed.

About a year later, when war was raging, the Colonel was leading a team with a mission to remove hundreds of American rebels who had taken over the Pittsburgh airport. There were four Canadian and twenty-seven American military squads surrounding the airport as dawn broke.

When the hundred or so rebels awoke, they were greeted by thousands of soldiers in full gear, with guns pointing at them from every angle. Some ran back inside the nearest buildings to hide, others surrendered without putting up a fight. Countless men and women lifted their guns to shoot, but were instantly shot first.

One tall, awkward man stood out. He was taking tiny steps backwards, trying to slip away without attracting any attention. His head was lowered, but Amica didn't need a clear look at his face to know exactly who was in front of her.

There stood the very man who violated her, Andrew Pratt. His shoulders seemed exceptionally bulky for his narrow waist. He was well over six feet tall, maybe closer to seven, and trotted clumsily. He was always slightly slouched forward, except that one awful night. He stood perfectly erect when he thrust himself violently into her body, a torture he most likely forced onto many women.

Who knew how many there had been before her?

The Colonel's blood boiled while she watched him attempting to sneak away yet again. *Not this time*, the words echoed loudly in her head. Colonel Harrison instructed her troops to detain him, and as the command was issued, Andrew bolted towards the large airport hub.

Amica's feet flew even faster than his. She was gaining on him and was within inches as he reached for the handle of the building's entrance. After quickly assessing the back of his large pointy ears and confirming he was in fact her rapist, she stopped.

Amica cocked her gun and pointed it at the base of his skull. She screamed for a halt and the troops around her froze. The devil in a camouflage jumpsuit did not obey and continued to swing open the door. No hesitation, not giving a second thought. Amica pulled the trigger not once, but thrice.

Bang, through his back, directly into his heart. Again in his head as he fell, and the third right between the legs as he slumped onto the cement. The Colonel's team remained motionless as she walked over, confirmed he was dead, and then continued to detain the next closest rebel inside the airport. Later, she said that he went for his gun. That's why she commanded him to halt, and then fired when he didn't comply.

Although Amica never paid any legal or military consequences for her actions, the memory still haunted her. Intinitally it gave her an overwhelming burst of pride and satisfaction, then guilt, and finally a hole that wouldn't close. Colonel Harrison knew it wouldn't solve Rose's grief, yet dulling the pain temporarily was the only gift she could offer.

"Rose, I promise you that he won't hurt anyone else. That man will get what is coming to him, but it's not going to make your anger go away." The Colonel reached for her hand, but Rose's arms remained folded at her chest.

"He must die. Please. Let. Me. Kill. Him." Rose was relentless.

Silence spread through the room as the two fierce women stared each other down. The highly-emotional motionless minute was finally broken when the Colonel's wristband alert went off. The image on the screen confirmed their package had been delivered.

"Will you settle for watching him kill himself?" Amica's smirk grew into a beaming smile as she watched Rose's reaction.

"Yes!" Rose answered without hesitation. She was so excited that she hugged Amica, a physical gesture rarely shared without asking for permission first. "Sorry, wait, how exactly are you going to make that happen?"

"Let me show you." The Colonel gestured for Rose, Matt, and Josée to follow her outside.

In the parking lot, there was a burly truck driver standing next to a flatbed truck, stacked with thirty-six-by-six-feet slabs of thick, solid rubber. Each piece had holes drilled in the same width apart as the wall poles and a metal frame that would hold the exterior piece firmly.

There was also a machined ledge that had hinges attached to one side. Behind the trucker stood a crane with a crew to install their new shield.

"Based on the trajectory, his grenade barely cleared two feet above the wall. This shield should create an added barrier that deflects anything he sends back in his direction. We will add this piece on our side along the border, send the drone out, and watch what happens next." The Colonel secretly prayed her plan would actually work.

The team quietly erected the first three barriers, closed the hinges, and secured the cap on each pole with a fast-drying adhesive. Ideally, they didn't want it tested immediately, but the drone was foreshadowing a faster conclusion. They watched Dixon on the other side of the wall, stroking the grenade and fondling the slingshot. Another strike appeared imminent.

The crane had lifted the fourth guard in place, only a few feet from where Amica, Josée, Matt, and Rose were standing. Rose was watching the footage from the drone, hopping from one foot to the next in youthful anticipation. Her heart raced as she watched her mother's murderer pull the grenade back, cradled inside the same slingshot that stole such a precious life.

"Get back! He's doing it now!" Rose screamed, and they quickly moved further away from the wall. The crane operator parked his crane and descended the stairs. Rose was staring at the screen, eyes fixated as she scurried further away.

"It's in the air, out of my sight." They stopped simultaneously nearly forty feet away from the wall, far east of where the grenade was headed. Everyone stared at the new shield, which appeared motionless and secure.

An ear ringing explosion went off as they stood frozen by shock. They could see the smoke rising from within the wall. It must have fallen through the poles before reaching the shield and exploded on the ground between the tires. The cement within the surrounding tires cracked, but had nowhere to go, so remained tight inside the rubber tires. One center pole fell and a few others had splits, but that was it.

"He's pissed! He just climbed up, saw the minimal damage, and is now getting ready to send another one," Rose continued with the play by play, watching the drone images projecting from her wristband as the group slowly backed away even further. "The second one is in the air, higher than the last."

They waited in silence again, eyes focused on the new addition to the oddly-shaped wall. The Colonel thought she saw a small shift in one spot, but didn't vocalize her wishful thinking. Seconds later, there was another loud explosion, this time farther away, as the sound was muffled through the rubber and plastic barrier.

"I think we did it. It looked like he screamed in the air as his bomb fell next to him. It instantly burst into a fiery explosion. He's not moving." Rose beamed at the thought of victory and then her voice quietly trailed off. The group stood still for minutes as they each internally processed what had occurred. Life was lost due to a choice they made.

Rose's excitement faded faster than the Colonel anticipated. She saw it in her eyes, and wasn't surprised when the kind-hearted young woman broke the silence by whispering, "Please say I didn't just kill someone?"

"You didn't. He threw the grenade. He killed himself." Colonel Harri gave Rose's hand a soft squeeze. "This was the only outcome that would allow us to continue without fear."

The Colonel walked back towards their golf course home, chatting with Rose along the way.

"Now that the threat is gone, I need Josée on board a ship that's about to sail. I want to work with the production team on improving security along the entire southern border. I apologize that I need to run so soon, but I promise I'll be back. If you're interested, I'd love for you to lead the new border patrol team we're creating."

"Yes! I would love that, Colonel. Anything you need, I'm willing. Shooting shit bombs was kind of fun." Rose's expression went from sad, to happy, then quickly to sad again. "Thank you for coming here, and for getting rid of that asshole."

"I didn't do it alone. We're in this together. We're a team, Rose. Thank you," Colonel Harrison replied sincerely.

One problem was solved for now, but there was still so much that had to be done to prevent another life from being tragically lost. The Colonel motioned to Josée to grab her gear, waved goodbye to the Fort Wayne bunch, and they took off in their two-seater POP to Tallahassee.

The Ship has Sailed

Josée volunteered to be a passenger on the ship to Australia to ensure the crew returned safely without any unwanted extra passengers. They created an elaborate backstory for her, claiming she was a socialite from Toronto who married a wealthy American that was killed in a robbery. It was eerily close to Josée's own personal story, yet she showed no emotion as Colonel Harrison filled her in on who she was supposed to be for the next few weeks.

"Most of your wealth is secure in American corporate ventures and gold. The online profile we created implies you have a hair trigger, explosive temper, and have killed people simply for getting too close. Don't be afraid to get nasty if necessary. You can't show any weakness or they will take advantage of you," Amica explained.

"Bryan will act as Captain John's bodyguard and stay in the cockpit with him, plus there will be five guards watching the supplies and prisoners. Tamika will be in the cabin next to you, which will have an access door between them. Publicly, you should act like you don't know or trust one another," She continued.

"There are also seven crew members on board, who do not know the whole truth about Australia. Captain John will fill them in once the passengers have left the ship.The fewer people who know on board during the voyage, the less chance of the plot being spoiled before you reach the shore."

The Colonel went over the extensive details for the first hour of their flight, and then switched to quizzing her for the remainder of their trip. She transferred an alert post with a summary of the various stories used to create both Josée and Tamika's profiles for their reference on the ship.

"It'll be a long trip. There is ample food on board and a revolver hidden in a safe under your bed. The combination is 061979; it's in the encrypted file. Captain John will be armed as well, in case anyone causes trouble. Do you have any concerns or questions?" The Colonel asked once they landed.

"How are we going to celebrate when your master plan comes to fruition?" Josée inquired with a bright, toothy smile.

"I already have a few kegs scheduled with an Ontario brewery that is still operational. We'll have a big party waiting for your return. Please make sure you come back to celebrate with us." The Colonel swallowed any signs of fear that they wouldn't have reason to celebrate.

"You've got it, boss!" Josée gave a quick salute, exited the plane, and walked towards the makeshift port. The Colonel disappeared into the clouds before she could be seen.

A massive carrier ship tied to an old metal gate using thick cables bobbed gently in the water. There was no dock leading to the boat, so passengers had to wade waist-deep to a rope ladder slung over the side. People with power and money were not used to the inconvenience and were vocal as Josée approached the scene solo.

"I'm wearing four hundred-dollar shoes which are now ruined. This trip better improve once we're on that boat!" A lanky man in a full suit with the legs rolled up past his knees grumbled as he made his way to the ship's ladder.

Although wading didn't bother Josée in the least, she jumped into the role of a disgusted elitist. She marched up to where the water lapped onto the concrete beach, put her hands on her hips, and shouted, "There had better be a little boat taking me to the bigger boat, or someone is carrying me on to that ship."

A stunning redhead in a navy fitted romper with gold accents approached Josée. Her hands were clasped together as she gently advised the undercover asset, "We deeply apologize, Madame, but this was the closest we could get the ship to shore. There is no rush to board, as we are waiting on a few other passengers. I think we have rubber boots you could wear, if you would like."

"Wear someone else's boots? I don't think so. Was my luggage delivered? I have proper water shoes in my beach bag. Please fetch them." Josée didn't want to be demanding of the crew, especially this breath-taking beauty. The bitchiness felt right for the role.

"Are they inside your on-board suitcases or your secure trunk?" The helpful stewardess probed further.

"I'm not sure, please check both. They're solid black rubber slip-ons." Josée only had minutes to decide what she was bringing before they took off to Indiana. Royelle finished packing her belongings after she left and had them sent on her behalf.

"I can only check your room; the rest is locked and guarded until we're safely docked. May I have the key to your room to retrieve your shoes?" She suggested generously.

Captain John had her key, and was supposed to slip it to her discreetly. Josée didn't like the idea of a stranger rifling through her belongings, even if she was someone on the B.E.S.T. team. She would feel bad if the shoes weren't there, and how would she explain why the Captain had her key? Josée wasn't even on the ship yet, and it appeared she was already overplaying her hand.

"Fucking forget it!" Josée shouted. She took off her shoes, tossed them in her reusable sack, and stormed into the water. The ground beneath her must have been a road or a cement pad, because it felt too smooth to have been made by Mother Nature. She scaled the rope in seconds and began her search for the Captain.

Captain John was an exceptionally large man, standing six foot, seven inches, with arms wider than Josée's thighs. His bodyguard Bryan was half the size, but his tanned muscles bulged from beneath his shirt. The Captain was physically blocking the entrance to the cockpit with his body while Bryan paced in front, eyeing every passenger as they made their way to their assigned cabin.

"*Bonjour, Madame.* Are you excited for our journey to the Gold Coast?" Bryan greeted her as if they had never met.

"*Oui, Monsieur.* I hear Australia is the place to be and it can't be the place to be without me," Josée continued their rehearsed introduction.

"I must agree, *aussi,*" Bryan replied. The Colonel suggested throwing the odd French word as a sign to one another that they felt safe and had no concerns. Spanish meant there was potential for trouble and dirty words in Italian meant danger was approaching quickly.

"I'm sorry to bother the Captain, but they told me yesterday at check-in that the Captain would hold my thyroid and migraine medication in his quarters until my arrival. My head is splitting already." Josée touched her temple to sell the excuse.

"Ah yes, Josée, we have your purse in our safe. One moment, *Madame.*" Captain John, turned around, retrieved the black zipper case from the safe, and handed it to Josée.

They had to play this game, rather than have the Captain just hand Josée the key, because she missed the security screening process the day prior. Every person was instructed to arrive the day before to drop off their belongings. They were told to arrive with nothing on their person except the plastic key card that unlocked their rooms. The bags they selected for inside the rooms were not allowed to contain anything that could be used as a weapon.

What the passengers didn't know was that those belongings never made it onto the ship destined for 'paradise,' or as the Colonel nicknamed, the 'Badlands.' Everything that was supposed to be stored in the hull was actually placed onto another ally ship, headed to a port in Quebec.

The Colonel made arrangements for a steel company to melt down the weapons and sell the steel at a significant discount to a company that produced wind energy and solar panels for wealthier Canadians. In exchange for the cost savings, the wind tower company committed to tearing down one abandoned building and replacing it with trees for every environmental energy system they sold.

This sparked a trade initiative that resulted in converting two former industrial complexes back into six hundred acres of thriving forests in the first two years. One forest was located in Montreal and the other in Toronto, two of the few Canadian cities that still had a functioning economy. The ghostly skyscrapers came down and were replaced with smaller, spread out homes powered by solar panels and miniature wind towers.

Instead of everyone's precious cargo, the hull had the two handcuffed prisoners who threatened the Colonel and her team in Michigan, as well as three guards armed with stun guns and enough supplies for the four of them to survive the trip. Once the passengers were all safely off the boat, the three guards inside the storage area would force the prisoners inside two large trunks.

Every part of the plan had the potential for mortal danger.

Back at Base Camp

Once her initial plans to protect and preserve the earth around them were running smoothly, it was time for the Colonel to build a unified society. Not everyone inside the wall had signed the agreement, as hundreds of thousands were already living within its border. The Canadian population was impacted the least from the various wars, pandemics, and destructive climate change, and there were Canadian citizens scattered from coast to coast.

Amica made sure the media spread both campaigns thoroughly throughout Canada, and no one protested the wall's construction. Only seven Canadians purchased the trip to Australia, and after reviewing their hate-filled online profiles, Amica thought, *Good riddance to rubbish.*

Although things seemed to be functioning well inside their manufactured bubble, the Colonel understood how important structure would be to their continued survival. More than half of those inside were earning some form of pay and were following the old way of business. The remainder were working for free in exchange for food, shelter, and a sense of community.

The Colonel felt she couldn't possibly speak on behalf of everyone, and created a campaign to encourage feedback from the community. She broke it down into three sections: an opportunity to vote, a survey, and a future career assessment. Her growing list of media contacts and social influencers spread the link like wildfire.

EVERY VOICE MATTERS

We're rebuilding the world and we can't do it successfully without your input. Please fill in as much or as little as you're comfortable sharing. Make sure your contact information is filled in and the agreement signed if you'd like to join the B.E.S.T. community workforce.

PICK YOUR PREFERENCE FOR THE FOLLOWING

Vote for the guidelines our citizens will follow by selecting one of two or three specified options. It is essential to our principles of

B.E.S.T.

balance, equity, stability, and teamwork that we share the same general priorities and sense of responsibility.

1. What type of society appeals to you most?
    a. Socialist Community Collaboration
    b. Communist Dictatorship
    c. Traditional Democratic Governance
2. What's more important to your quality of life?
    a. Right to own a gun
    b. Freedom from guns
3. Does cash or currency matter if there's no authority enforcing its value?
    a. Yes
    b. No
4. Are you willing to follow the B.E.S.T. rules as stated in this link?
    a. Yes
    b. No
5. What should the punishment be for breaking a B.E.S.T. rule?
    a. Immediate Exile
    b. Confinement based on severity
    c. One warning; exile on second offense.
    d. Execution
6. Do you believe our planet can be saved?
    a. Yes
    b. No
    c. I'm not convinced, but am willing to try.
7. Are you willing to work in exchange for food and the support of the B.E.S.T. alliance?
    a. Yes
    b. No

SHARE YOUR IDEAS

Please tell us what you think inside the comment box next to each question.

1. Describe your ideal utopia using only three words.
2. Name the top three things you need to survive.
3. Describe one way you can help repair our environment.

4.   Name three qualities you look for in a leader.

5.   Describe your most valued physical or personal asset.

6.   Name three foods you could not live without.

7.   Describe something you miss from before war broke out.

BUILD YOUR FUTURE

Under the four principles of B.E.S.T., there are countless roles required for our future success. Please answer the following questions to tell us how you can contribute to B.E.S.T.'s workforce. We believe job satisfaction comes from choosing the career you want, and as long as you are capable, your role within B.E.S.T. can differ from your educational background.

1. Out of the four principles of B.E.S.T., which is most important to you?
   a. Balance - Reduce environmental and political threats
   b. Equity - Redistribution of wealth and resources equally
   c. Stability - Ensuring progress can be maintain and sustained
   d. Teamwork - Collaboration and participation from all members

2. Which role at B.E.S.T. would be your first choice?
   a. Forest & Water Restoration
   b. Resource Procurement & Fulfillment
   c. Marketing & Communications
   d. Farming & Meal Prep
   e. Strategy & Security
   f. Material Handling & Delivery
   g. Emergency & Medical Services

3. Please select any of the following fields where you have education or experience that you would like to use.
   a. Environmental Science or Engineering
   b. Medical and/or Health Sciences
   c. Community outreach or Communications
   d. Manufacturing - especially mold making or 3-D design
   e. Agriculture and/or Culinary Arts

       f.   Political or Legal Representation

4.   Please select your greatest asset that you would want to utilize in a future role.

       a.   Innovative/Intelligence

       b.   Intuition/Proactiveness

       c.   Speed/Physical strength

       d.   Creativity/Imagination

       e.   Personality/Charm

       f.   Healer/Mediator

5.   Choose the option that best describes your ideal work environment.

       a.   You as Manager, overseeing everything

       b.   Working under a Manager who's double-checking everything

       c.   Working solo, with support available when requested

       d.   Part of a team, working together equally

6.   Where would you prefer to work?

       a.   Inside the Trenton Base

       b.   Inside Algonquin Park

       c.   In a farmer's field.

       d.   Near my current location (please specify)

             —————————————————

       e.   Along the border wall

       f.   Anywhere I'm needed

7.   Are you willing to work for a minimum of thirty hours per week in exchange for shared resources and protection?

       a.   Yes

       b.   No

Thousands of surveys were filled in within minutes of being sent, dumping the data into a growing spreadsheet. The Colonel asked Arturo, his assistant Ashley, Commander Ying, and Kali to go through the responses and work with each applicant on finding a suitable role based on their answers and personal career interests.

The Colonel and Supreme Minister Forte tasked themselves with sorting through any survey results that set off red flags. They were looking for threats among them, like gun lovers who felt execution was a reasonable response to breaking the rules.

This Ass is Off-Limits

Josée and Tamika were trying their best to blend in and get along, but the men were getting restless by the sixth day on the water. Inside B.E.S.T. and most of Canada, women were in leading positions and had a fair say at the table. Gender seemed almost irrelevant.

The ship did not share that same balance. Most of the passengers were elite,arrogant men, overwhelmingly caucasian. It was a distinction evident to both women, whose skin tones were rich blends of several ethnicities. Interracial marriage and procreation, accompanied by a thin ozone layer and fierce sun, meant no one looked white anymore regardless of race. The pale faces of untanned men stood out, especially unmasked.

Starting with the pandemic in 2020, it became a considerate custom to wear a mask whenever traveling or celebrating in large groups. People would instinctively cover their mouths and noses to protect themselves and others when they were inside a large venue, an airplane, or watercraft that held more than a dozen people. The B.E.ST. team members tucked their masks away when they noticed no one else on the ship was wearing one.

The female crew stood out even more so, and were instantly targets of aggressive flirting and harassment, followed by violent threats if the men were rejected. Both women had developed thick skins over their challenging lives and ignored it the best they could.

That was, until ignoring it was no longer an option.

"Lady, why do you wear such baggy tops? I can tell you have a tight little body. Let us appreciate how good it looks, or even better, how nice it feels." A large-nosed, greasy man stopped Josée on her way up to the deck, blocking her passageway.

"I like there to be some mystery. You need to earn the right to see this body," Josée quickly fired back, hunching her shoulders forward, to minimize her breasts.

"I have the right to do whatever I want, and I want to suck on those perky nipples." His mouth widened with each word, showing off his coffee-stained teeth. "Who's going to stop me?"

"Considering I also have the right to do what I want, I just won't let you see this body." Josée darted underneath the arm he was using to prop himself up against the wall. She poked him under his rib cage with the sharp point of her elbow. The agile, avid runner scurried up the stairs to the main deck, but not fast enough to miss his reply.

"Feminist bitch. We're not done," He muttered, motionless, staring after her like prey that had barely escaped his grasp.

That first incident of the flirtation turning nasty sparked the regular harassment of Josée from all sides, and any woman she went near. The greaseball with the distinctive nose joined forces with several other homely men to taunt and crowd the women whenever they ventured outside of their cabins.

"I'd love to take a slow drive along your curves," One plump man called out to Tamika when she went to pick up their midday nutrients and edibles.

"I'm seasick and you're the cure," Another whispered as Josée walked by when she simply went on deck to soak up a little sunlight.

"My cabin or yours, my lady?" A heavy-set stranger asked, while scooping Tamika's hand into his own. She yanked it back and shook her head back and forth, pushing herself past him. The death stares they shot back in return didn't make enough of an impact to prevent future harassment.

The slick guy with the big nose, who she later learned was appropriately named Cyrano, popped up everywhere Josée went. She'd turn a corner, he'd be standing there, intentionally pressing his body into hers before passing by, the back of his hands or the tips of his fingers probing her ass cheeks in the exchange.

Josée clenched her jaw and accepted the abuse at first. Women were significantly outnumbered on the ship and she couldn't formulate an appropriate response without first securing male allies. The ladies checked their exact stats with Captain John and were shocked. Out of the two hundred and sixty-three paying passengers on the ship, only twenty-nine were women.

Gender was almost completely irrelevant in Canada prior to Canadian Prime Minister Kait Schwartz's assisination. Her first policy change was removing gender from every government form and questionnaire. PM Schwatz's campaign was won on her platform to eliminate distinct gender definitions, and most say that was the very same reason she was killed.

Even after her death, being the only woman in a sea of men wouldn't have mattered in Canada. Most people couldn't distinguish anyone else's linear classification. Society had shattered stereotypes, as interracial and bisexual relationships melded everyone into a beautiful blend of one another. No one could be certain of your ethnicity or your gender based on mere appearance, nor did it matter.

On a boat full of wealthy white men, caramel-skinned women were the noticeable minority.

This was not the first time Josée faced unbelievable odds and rose above them. Her life was once peaceful, ordinary, and simple. That was just the way Josée used to like things to be. She moved from Amherstburg to Michigan for her nursing job in 2026, before the second pandemic broke out. Soon after starting her new job, she met Aiden, a sous-chef at a local restaurant. They married in 2028 and her life felt complete.

One cold January night in 2035 changed everything. The happy couple met after work at a craft brewery near their home for a pint. They both worked the evening shift; it was almost midnight and they only had the energy for one beer before calling it a night. They held hands as they sauntered home, swinging their arms dramatically between them in an effort to generate a little heat.

Josée couldn't stop smiling.

Click. Pppssst. Ting. Thud. A click followed by air slowly seeping out, a tiny zing, and then the full weight of his body crashing onto the ground on top of her. His arm pulled Josée underneath him as he fell. Aiden lay over her like a shield. Josée felt his warm blood ooze onto her as he protected her from the gunfire that ensued.

Josée laid beneath Aiden until she faded into the blissful ignorance between sleep and sunrise. When her eyelids finally separated hours later, she was a widow afraid of her own shadow. She crawled home, locked her door, and told no one what happened.

She stayed indoors the first four days, barricading her windows and searching for ways to get back inside Canada. The Windsor-Detroit border had been temporarily closed after a bomber blew up the bridge earlier that ear, and although the tunnel was intact, the government kept it closed due to the raging spread of both war and deadly viruses that was plaguing the United States.

Being frightened by the gun violence and war surrounding her and frustrated Canada wouldn't let her back into her home country lit an inferno inside Josée. She stopped going to work and began training herself on self-defense techniques and strategies. Her physical statute was small, and her studies suggested using intimidation to appear larger. The advice was to act fearless and almost crazed as a way of deterring threatening individuals from approaching.

A gleeful snort slipped out when Josée recalled the first time practicing her new personality in public. She was thirty-one years old, sick of sitting inside hating the world, and desperately wanting to venture onto her porch with confidence. She put on a pair of baggy yellow pajama pants, a tight, ripped black tank top, and oversized sunglasses. It was the middle of February.

Although her skin felt cold enough to crack, Josée didn't flinch. She lit a fat joint, put one hand on her hip, and squinted her eyes as if she was staring down someone in disgust. She stood outside for over an hour, unwavering. If anyone returned her dirty look or attempted to approach her, she muttered loudly, "God's gonna get ya. God's gonna get ya."

The next day, she upped her game by walking to the corner store, swinging a reusable bag full of rocks and chatting, "Only God can cast stones. Only God. God's gonna get ya, only God." People would cross the street just to avoid her.

No one made Josée feel like a victim ever again. She joined the military a few months later, was quickly promoted into special forces, and was now a lethal weapon used to torture terrorists and manipulate powerful people. There was no way she'd allow the men on the boat to abuse her without fighting back. She knew the weapons she had hidden were only to be used as a last resort, or in self-defense. Josée was looking for a reason to justify putting a bullet into several of the aggressive men's skulls.

Keeping her anger in check, she thought about what the Colonel might suggest as a non-violent response. How could two women intimidate or gain control over countless men? What advantage did they have that they could use to exploit the men's greatest disadvantage?

The majority of passengers on the boat had plans to repopulate, which would be even more challenging than they realized, considering four of the women would be returning with the ship to Canada. Nine of the remaining women were over the average of forty and a few others were the wives and girlfriends of the flirtatious passengers who had yet to bear any children of their own.

The only single and potentially available women on the ship consisted of one plastic surgeon, three lawyers, and two socialite sisters who made millions as social influencers. Josée and Tamika came up with a strategy where they would leverage their working ovaries to keep them alive.

"Do these assholes realize if they keep treating the few women available like shit, they'll end up alone and childless in Australia," Josée pondered out loud. The two women were in the habit of meeting behind the locked door of their cabin in the early evenings before the house settled down for the night.

"Maybe we need to make the men want our wombs rather than our vaginas? We are their best bet on ever having a baby." Tamika brought up the suggestion as a way they could survive the next few weeks.

"How can we use our baby-making abilities to keep the guys off of us? Bringing up that we're potential breeders could make the rape attempts more frequent." Josée bit her lip, searching for a more suitable solution.

"I think it's all in how we say it. We could explain that we're selective and waiting to see which man builds the most desirable future for both ourselves and the next generation. We're saving ourselves for procreation," Tamika exclaimed, pouring out the idea that had been brewing since their last bull session. "We'll decide which man gets to swim inside our fertile eggs thirty days after we land and no one can have us any sooner."

"I can sell that." Her petite friend nodded along.

"I've used it on dates before, why not now?" The more formidable-sized woman confessed.

"You're a fucking genius, Tamika!" Josée shouted "They've got to earn this ass."

"Shouldn't they always?" The ebony-skinned beauty clapped back.

"Yes, but this caliber of men doesn't understand boundaries. This way, they'll be fighting over us while we're sailing back to utopia. It's worth a try to put an end to the constant harassment." Josée was eagerly awaiting the chance to strand these self-serving men permanently.

These wise ladies realized they could twist their disadvantage into their favor, simply by playing on the lack of available females. Getting pregnant might not have been the joyous occasion it once was, due to the sad state of the world, however, rebuilding a civilization on a 'thriving' continent would be most men's long-term goal. The ability to create future generations was a prized commodity.

With massive grins, the women set their plan into motion.

"I plan on having a child once we are settled, and only one at that. That privilege won't go to someone who grabs my ass every time I pass by. This ass is off-limits until someone treats me the way I deserve," Josée loudly scolded the very next man who groped her bottom as she squeezed by him in a narrow, bright white corridor.

Tamika said something similar to another aggressive male shortly afterwards, and they continued their line of defense until they successfully flipped the script. The men suddenly stepped back to allow the women enough room to move freely. They rushed to pull out their chairs in the dining room, and offered the ladies portions of their limited rations. A few still got too close or would 'accidentally' brush against them, but their demeanor lacked the previous stench of entitlement.

With the exception of the first week or so, the thirty-nine days on the ship were relatively uneventful. The only problems were a few passengers trying to subtly sneak a feel, one man whipping out his limp penis while reeling from opioids he had snuck on board, and another guest threatening to throw a man overboard after losing a 'friendly' wager. The attempted murder was avoided when Josée and Tamika separated and distracted both men long enough for tempers to cool. Balance was restored on the trip and they could travel without living in fear.

Maybe a little more than just balance was restored for Tamika.

Her faith in men was rebounding, though she was never one to expect a man to rescue her. Tamika was raised by a fierce feminist mother and an unconditionally supportive father. She was taught to stand her own ground, whether up against a man or a woman. Tamika wasn't sure how she felt about Passenger twenty-one, Mr. William H.

Jefferson, who jumped to her defense when another man was being a bit too hands-on.

"I asked you kindly to apologize to this lady and keep your hands off her body in the future," A stern, yet silky-smooth voice responded to a man squeezing her bum cheek as he went by, before Tamika had a chance to process another violation.

Tamika was almost six feet tall, but William towered over her. His lean muscular physique, vibrant blue eyes, and full lips created an instant chemical attraction. Her look of disgust towards the first man turned into a smile directed at the second.

"Thank you, but I would have told him where to go. I'm saving this body for someone who wants to raise a family in the new world," Tamika recited the storyline they were generating.

"I've seen you hold your own already; you must be tired of fighting the same battles with all of these pervy men on board. I like being a good guy, someone needs to show women that we're not all immature pigs. It was my sincere pleasure," William replied.

"I know they are still good guys on this earth, but how can I be certain that you're one of the good ones? You could be playing Prince Charming to get into my pants. I've fallen for that one more than once. I am a hell of a lot wiser now." Tamika always assumed everyone had a hidden agenda, as that was the lesson life taught her.

"I'm twice your size and could get into those pants whether you let me or not. But, I assure you, I'd never try without your blessing," He pushed back.

"As if you would say otherwise?" Tamika smirked.

"When you and your friend go to bed at night, the guys around here help themselves to anything they want, including some of the other women. If you weren't locked in your room, they'd try the same. They watch each other behaving like depraved animals. No one cares about the poor woman being publicly abused and humiliated. I could never do that to anyone, nor can I stand to stomach the sight of it. I also don't need to prove that to you," William stated sternly, though it still wasn't enough to convince Tamika.

"Am I supposed to appreciate that you're not a rapist? Is that an achievement worth bragging about? You have the human decency not to assault another human being, but you still allow it to happen without trying to stop it! Wow, you're awesome." Sarcasm was her strong suit, and she wielded it like a Samurai sword.

"In a world where no one cares what you do or who you hurt, keeping my hands to myself is a sign of respect. I don't care who you sleep with, or if one day it will be me; that's not my motive. I do not choose to stay silent if I see someone abusing someone else, however I'm vastly outnumbered on this ship. What do you expect me to do?" William fought back.

"Yeah, guess it's too much to ask men to stop other men from raping women. It'd be nice if we could get men to stop abusing us in the first place, maybe give women a chance to exist without constant harassment and sexual advances. Obviously, that's too much to ask." Tamika swung her imaginary sword of truth, slicing through his excuses.

"There was a time when I would have intervened, and I hope there will be a time again when I can stop it from being such a regular occurrence for far too many women. Right now I can't, and that bothers me deep in my soul. I wish things were different." William went from enraged to meek and defeated.

He followed his confession with a quick "ood day, Ma'am" and disappeared below deck.

Their first verbal exchange opened the door to more regular conversations. They would seek each other out and chat about random topics to pass the time. Tamika was surprised by his compassion and that they shared similar political beliefs. He felt guns were necessary for hunting and protection, but never considered himself a gun enthusiast until after the United States of America had officially divided.

One afternoon, while discussing how dark and cloudy the ocean looked, she took her chance to find out how a decent man ended up on the ship destined for the 'Badlands.' William was comparing the water to a sink full of dirty dishes and how important it was to remove all objects contributing to the filth before straining the water from the impurities. Tamika knew he would be an asset to B.E.S.T., and was heartbroken that she'd soon be abandoning him on a barren island.

"I want to ask you something, William, and I need a real, honest answer. What made you take this route, instead of joining the rebuilding efforts in the north? You don't seem to share the same point of view as most of the other passengers," She asked quietly, while looking deep into his eyes.

"Neither do you. What made you take this chance?" He twisted the question back onto her.

"I'm strong and resilient, but every day is a battle when you're a woman with money. I figured there would be fewer people trying to steal from me if everyone else was financially secure." That was Tamika's conservative version of her true beliefs. In a truly equitable society, violence wouldn't be necessary.

"Alright, guess that makes sense. I felt the same. I was tired of seeing savages beat and abuse one another. My size was enough to intimidate most, but I was always jumping in to help others. It's exhausting being a referee, and my inclination to intervene has already rewarded me with two painful gunshots. I might not survive the next one." Tamika stared deep into his eyes as he spoke; his sincerity was unmistakable.

"That's awful. Where were you shot?" She asked while holding firmly to their intense eye contact.

"The first time was in Detroit, June third, 2039, when I was fighting on behalf of the North State Community. The second was last month when I took on some punk who was robbing a young lesbian couple at gunpoint. He saw the pair of women kissing on a bench, called them nasty names, pulled out his gun, and demanded their purses. I grabbed him from behind, but he jammed the gun in my gut and pulled the trigger before I could stop him." William lifted his shirt, exposing a gnarly scar and rock-hard body.

"Oh my, William. That sounds scary. What did you do?" Her mind raced trying not to tear up over his heroic and traumatizing experience.

"I turned his gun around before I passed out and shot him in the heart. The lovely ladies on the bench rushed me to an emergency health station and took turns staying by my side until I felt well enough to take care of myself. I'm getting old. I won't win the next standoff," The gentle giant explained as streams of tears collected on his cheeks.

"Wow, what an incredible story. You're a hero!" Tamika exclaimed, instinctually grabbing his hand in hers.

"That's the story that made me bet every cent I had on pursuing a better way of life." His obvious kindness and good nature poked guilt in her gut. She let go of his hand, well aware that his investment wouldn't work out the way he hoped.

"Wait, you fought on the North State Community side?" Tamika blindly assumed every paying passenger came from the New United Republic. Josée told her later on that the ship had a few Canadians and NSC originals who hadn't crossed into Canada when the Southern Rebels attacked in 2040.

"Yes, I was a Democrat, then an NSC member. Unfortunately, their hearts were bigger than their brains. They never had a defense or finance plan, it was only about social inclusion and fixing the environment. They left us vulnerable, and that's why more than half of the NSCs were killed so quickly. They weren't prepared to protect us," William sighed with the final word.

"I see." Tamika nodded slowly in agreement, realizing the Colonel's system for dividing the world based on their core values left out a major portion of the population: those who carried beliefs from both sides.

St. Paul's Balls

The Colonel continued her flight along the new border, checking in with the few team members who chose to stay close by. There was no one directly on the southern side of the wall until they reached St. Paul, Minnesota. Amica saw a few dozen people scattered around five mobile homes, three tents, a truck, and two POPs that were camped out about one hundred feet from the wall.

They didn't look particularly suspicious, but she could see damage was done to two of the poles and there was what appeared to be a black blast zone a foot or so in front of the broken pole. Amica swooped over the wall before anyone on the other side noticed and lowered herself onto the front lawn of the seven men living on the B.E.S.T. side of St. Paul.

Ox, David, Ryan, Jaxe, Pete, Oliver, and T became a team of friends and lovers while building the wall and decided to set up a community they affectionately named St. Paul's Balls. When the Colonel landed, they were living it up with loud music and sangria. They discovered a functioning flea market earlier in the week and were dancing around in their new-to-them vintage clothing.

Modern clothes in the 2040s were simple cotton blends with elastic waistbands or cinched drawstrings rather than buttons or zippers. Most of these gents had on cut-off denim shorts and flowy or collared dress shirts, except the two men dancing in the center:Pete, who was wearing a fitted, red sparkly party dress with black thigh-highs, and Oliver, who had on a high-collared emerald green blouse with tight white dress pants and rhinestone cowboy boots. The sight filled Amica with an unfiltered joy she hadn't felt in years.

The Colonel waited inside the small plane for a moment, soaking up their carefree happiness while regretting her choice in attire. Her gray leggings and basic black top felt like a wet blanket compared to their vibrance.

"Good day, Gentlemen," She called out as she approached. She spent a bit of time with Oliver and met David at least once during the build. "Wonderful to see you again.or those who may not know, I am Colonel Amica Harrison."

Ryan jumped up to turn the radio off while Ox, David, T, and Pete instinctually stood at attention and formally saluted her, caught off-guard by her presence. Oliver smiled, continuing to sway his hips while giving the Colonel a slow, deliberate salute. "Welcome, Colonel. It's great to see you again."

"You as well, although I wish it was under better circumstances."

"Are we in danger?" Ryan's eyes widened as he asked.

"Did we do something wrong?" T questioned.

"It's not imminent danger, but there are outsiders possibly trying to make their way a few miles south of you," The Colonel explained what she witnessed from the POP, which matched their suspicions.

"We heard shots and an explosion a couple days after the attack in Fort Wayne. We fortified about a twenty-foot section using old siding strapped together with bungee cords. We slid the pieces between the poles on this side of the wall, so there's something extra to catch anything that attempts to get through," Ox advised.

"Smart. Very smart. There's equipment on its way now to build a higher shield along this section to deflect any explosives they attempt to toss over. It should be here in the next few days, but no one should take any chances in the meantime. I'd appreciate it if you'd gather your resources and head at least five miles north. Find a spot that is not so much in the open, stay quiet, and be on alert," The Colonel instructed.

"Someone is trying to bomb us?" Oliver questioned loudly.

"Possibly. Probably," Amica attempted to strike a balance between genuine concern and destructive panic.

"Does that mean no more listening to music and dancing in the streets?" Pete asked with a pout.

"Music is alright, just not so loud that you draw attention to yourself or wouldn't hear a bomb going off in the distance. I want you to enjoy your lives without fear, and you will again. This is just temporary until the shield is up. The first time they toss something your way and it bounces back should be enough to send them running in the opposite direction," Colonel Harrison calmly reassured the shaken group.

Amica smiled softly and made direct eye contact with each man individually as she patted her chest above her heart. It was a custom signifying a heartfelt connection that had replaced handshakes and hugs after the first global pandemic.

"We've been meaning to check out what's available further north anyway. Don't worry, Colonel, we will be on our way shortly," Oliver assured her with the same purposeful eye contact. He then clasped his hands in front of him in a partial prayer pose and said, "May our travels be swift and our arrivals safe."

"Our Border Security Officer Rose will notify you once it is safe to return. I have given her your connection signal. Please stay far away from the wall until she can properly secure it," The Colonel stressed yet again.

"We promise, Colonel. It's a big, wide open world on this side of the wall. I'm sure we'll find another magnificent space to call our home," Ryan promised.

"Swift travels and safe arrival. If you need anything, please send me a wrist alert," Amica responded sincerely.

They exchanged goodbyes and she was off again with only one more stop before returning to base camp. She was anxious to check on the ship's status. Royelle sent her updates that it was smooth sailing, but she knew Royelle wouldn't give her bad news until she was on solid ground.

When she arrived back at base, that uneasy feeling in her belly was first confirmed and then almost instantly dismissed. It wasn't great news; a wild animal snuck into their carrot and cabbage patch, devouring countless crops, but it could have been worse. The threat at the wall terrified her that she would lose another life tragically. Her heart was still broken over Melanie; Colonel Harrison refused to lose another team member under her command.

Three days later, the Colonel received a wrist alert from Officer Rose that the additional reflector pieces had been installed in St. Paul. Rose's message came through less than five hours before a massive blast. Somehow the group on the other side obtained a C4 rocket launcher and sent three rapid rounds in the wee hours of the morning. Each bomb bounced back, scattering the instant explosives among the gang who first cheered on their launch.

Whoosh, Hawhoosh, Kaplosh.

Pieces of their trailer accompanied by bone fragments were blown in every direction. Screams of agony echoed throughout the South. The threat had not only been averted, but word spread, and it frightened other terrorists from similar attempts. In fact, news of the attack increased legitimate enrollment in B.E.S.T. because it proved the leadership had effective strategies for keeping its community safe.

Not everything was perfect, but nothing was stopping their progress. They were bounding the hurdles and climbing over every obstacle. Colonel Harrison knew she could never let her guard down as long as she was in charge, but at the very least, she could rest knowing she was doing everything possible to keep the people who believed in her plan safe from harm. The tragedy of losing Melanie would not be repeated under her watch.

Bon Voyage, Suckers

After thirty-nine days on the water, Captain John could see the Australian coast through his periscope. As instructed by the Colonel, he activated the alert on his Command CellBand, which sent a signal to the other sixteen special free-loading passengers. This would instruct the crew members who weren't aware of the grand scheme to advise passengers that the ship was preparing to dock. Those in the know were to stand on guard to ensure everything went according to plan.

Josée was with Tamika when both their wrist bands began to vibrate. This meant they had less than an hour until the ship was securely docked and they could abandon the unwanted cargo on shore. Tamika went to her room to grab the switchblade and handcuffs she requested. The Colonel instructed her to pretend she was waiting for Bryan's help with her bags and to stand outside the control room, protecting Captain John.

As Tamika prepared herself physically and mentally, a sing-song rhythmic knock broke her concentration. Her gut could feel that it was William waiting on the other side, and this would be her last chance to tell him the truth.

"Tamika, it's William. Open up. Someone spotted the shoreline and people are packing up," His voice drifted through the door, prompting her to turn the handle mid-sentence.

"I'm still getting my stuff ready. We'll catch up on shore." Tamika couldn't hide the lack of enthusiasm in her response as the words dribbled out.

"I will wait for you. I want to make sure you're secure and safe because people will run amok once they're released from the ship and given their guns back. If you'll allow me to, I'd like to stick by your side, just in case I need to lift you over the crowds to get through." His genuine concern and charming smile made Tamika want to grab his face and embrace his full lips on hers.

"Carry me?" Tamika laughed. "I'm solid muscle; you're not lifting me over anything."

"I could and would." William's bright teeth beamed from between his lips.

"I'm sure that won't be necessary." Tamika attempted to push back, peering through the small crack she allowed it to open.

"I respect that you are a strong, self-sufficient woman, but I've heard men talking about what they're going to do once everyone has their luggage back. Some threats have been made and I believe they will be acted upon. I will gather my stuff and be back here in five minutes to get you. Don't leave without me, please," William pleaded with his chestnut brown puppy dog eyes.

"Wait, come inside. We need to talk." Tamika opened the door, then turned to sit on the edge of her bed. She gently padded the spot next to her. She couldn't leave him to die when he was so insistent on protecting her.

"What's wrong? Has someone else stolen your heart? That's all I'm after; I'm trying to earn your trust, my beautiful queen." He remained standing, towering over her, preparing for another heartbreak.

'Close the door," She instructed. He closed it and stepped closer to her.

"I'm not getting off the boat. I don't think you should, either." Tamika grabbed his large hand between both of hers, pulling him towards the spot next to her. "Listen, this isn't what you signed up for, and it's going to get way more ruthless in Australia then anything you experienced in the New Republic or the NSC. Trust me."

"What? I doubt they will let us stay on the ship. We spent the money and it's supposed to have anything we're lacking. I'm sure it will be fine. I will protect you," William attempted to reassure her through what he assumed was a last-minute panic attack.

"It's a trap. This trip was a giant ploy to remove the most dangerous gun enthusiasts from North America. The team at B.E.S.T., that's the new group rebuilding the north, worked with the Prime Minister of Australia to remove every asset and mode of transportation off of the shrinking, depleted continent. The ships holding everything that was valuable in Australia are currently docking in Vancouver. This trip was designed to leave every passenger stranded, fighting to their death," She rambled a quick synopsis, while William stared at her with a mystified expression.

She gave him a few more seconds to absorb and make sense of what she spewed before continuing, "I know it sounds wild, William, but it's kind of ingenious.There are a few hidden assets and crew members who will be staying on board. You can be one of them and become a member of B.E.S.T."

"Are you fucking serious? What about our supplies? The cargo that we dropped off the day before we left NUR?" William's smile transformed into a clenched jaw quite quickly.

"The only thing in the cargo haul are prisoners and rations for the ride home," Tamika explained.

"I can't believe this!" He shouted into the air, before turning to her with a quivering lip and asking, "Were you really going to leave me here to die?"

Tamika couldn't answer him. Moments earlier she was prepared to leave him there, in spite of their growing connection. William saw the hesitation and regret in her eyes, graciously deciding not to wait for her reply.

His expression softened ever so slightly before asking, "Why are you telling me this now?"

"I couldn't leave you here. I broke the Colonel's confidence in me, because I know you don't deserve to be stranded and killed. You truly want to rebuild a better world, and that's exactly what we're doing at B.E.S.T." Tamika turned to look directly in his eyes, hoping he'd see her sincerity.

"Why does anyone deserve to be stranded and killed?" His question punctured a hole in her plea, but Tamika didn't lose a beat.

"You just told me those men were threatening people's lives. You've seen them rape women. They will kill or rape me if given the chance; that's why you're insisting on protecting me and why I'm choosing to protect you. These people do not value any life other than their own, so I don't value theirs." Her soft tone penetrated his core. William began nodding in agreement.

Tamika waited for him to gather his belongings, so the crew didn't notice they had been left in his room. William agreed to wait in Tamika's room behind the locked door until she got back, after first reassuring him repeatedly that she had plenty of other people who would make sure she was safe.

In the next room, Josée located the safe with the gun, unlocked it, loaded the gun, and tucked it into her waistband. She gathered her carry-on, took a deep breath, and waited patiently on the inside of her estate room door. Twice someone knocked on the door, followed by, "We are preparing to dock. Please gather your belongings and head to the top deck."

She listened to loud cheers as a stampede of people marched eagerly past her door. A few called her name as they went by. Josée didn't make a sound. It took nearly thirty minutes for silence to fill the lower cabin. She peeked through the hole to confirm she was alone before opening the door.

The Colonel asked her to be on deck when the prisoners were escorted outside; it was the last step before they could all feel safe again. When Josée made her way to the top, she could see the last man hopping over the ledge to scale down the ladder onto the shore. She took her position at the top of the ladder, with her hand shoved inside her pants, fingers wrapped around the gun.

The shoreline was mostly peppered with men shouting for their precious cargo. Josée watched the hatch open below. One guard walked out and stood to the left, then four more appeared, two by two, carrying large wooden crates. The passengers rushed the guards as they lowered the crates onto the beach.

A guard put his hand up, halting the ensuing crowd. "Please take a few steps back and wait over there while we unload everyone's belongings. We still have more crates to unload and then we will release the cargo to each passenger. Only approach once your name has been called. It won't take long and it will still be another twenty minutes before your welcome wagon arrives. Please stand back."

There were a few grunts and sighs, but the passengers stopped their charge and watched as the guards made their way back up the ramp onto the ship's cargo bay. Just as the fifth guard boarded the ship, the lid popped open on one of the trunks.

"Stop the ship! They are leaving us here to die," One of the prisoners from Michigan sat up, screaming to the masses.

Another man lifted the lid of the other trunk and the two men began rambling about the Colonel's plan. One of the former military guards rapidly cranked the drawbridge for the ramp and Josée yanked the ladder up, drawing her gun on the group below.

"What the fuck are you doing? What's going on?!" A deep voice broke her concentration.

Josée recognized the arrogant, nasally voice immediately, and whipped around to find herself face-to-face with Cyrano. His massive hand grasped the gun below hers, yanking her arm into the air. He was over a foot taller, and he pulled her up onto her toes.

"You've been avoiding me and I didn't want you to slip away, especially since I plan on you giving me a son once we settle. I waited by the ladder, and when you didn't come, I went back down below. I found your room unlocked, your belongings still in it and you nowhere to be found." As the last word slipped from his mouth, the ship rocked enough for Cyrano to lose his balance.

"Is the ship moving?" He asked.

Both their hands were still on the gun, and the tall, more muscular man assumed he had the advantage. With his right hand still positioned below Josée's wrist, he placed his left hand on the edge of the boat, peering over at the men chasing, screaming, as the ship drifted back out. A moment of shock and pause, as his mind attempted to process exactly what was happening.

Without a second of hesitation, Josée dropped her left forearm, jammed her arm up between his legs, and hoisted his top-heavy body halfway over the edge. The pain of her solid arm crushing into his genitals took the wind out of his lungs, releasing his grip on the gun. His other fingers gripped tighter onto the railing, but one knee was now bent over the ledge, barely hanging on.

"Sorry, Cyrano, but this is your stop." Josée lifted the foot he still had on board, pushing it and the rest of his body overboard as she dipped her body under his. Gravity ripped his finger tips from their perch and he tumbled backwards into the rough waves cast from the ship. Splash. Josée watched his body bob up and down, arms waving, and then finally sinking about a mile away from where the other passengers were shouting.

Based on the desolate conditions Prime Minister Cortez left her once vibrant country in, Cyrano wasn't the only dead body on that shore. The rest just didn't know it yet.

Growing Gut Instinct

Colonel Amica Harrison had one stealthy skill that her life experiences had sharpened to a knifepoint: her intuition. Life had shown her that her instincts could be trusted, so if something felt off, she would go with her gut feeling. It was a vital skill that too many women ignored.

There was one person's survey result that appeared normal to everyone else, yet it was setting off alarms in her head. Alexia Hobes seemed too perfect and enthusiastically supportive, but at the same time, the Colonel sensed an undertone of anger. Another irregularity was how the signature resembled a cyberscript font rather than a handwritten scanned copy.

A landmark case in 2033 ruled against a four hundred million-dollar Vancouver contract that was signed during the third global pandemic since Covid first shook-up the world in 2020. The party purchasing the land, Mr. Pepperman, used a signature font in a PDF program rather than physically signing a hard copy and scanning it.

The agreement for a series of eight triplexes took place in 2028, when real estate pricing leveled off after a steady twelve-year climb in the housing market. The arrangement was for a contractor to fix up one row of townhouses at a time, aiming for two per year over the next four years.

The first unit was ready in 2029, but Mr. Pepperman couldn't find one renter, let alone three. The declining population, increasingly expensive resources, and involvement in various wars killed the housing market. When the second unit was ready, he insisted that he only agreed to purchase one. The seller couldn't prove the quantity wasn't changed after his electronic signature, or that the signature was in fact his, voiding the deal.

It was a shocking court case, accompanied by numerous articles on the importance of a handwritten signature and how to use your fingerprint and smart watch to sign a document quickly from your wrist. Most Canadians knew the story, and therefore wouldn't use the font option.

The survey ended up in her pile because the person specifically asked to work with the Colonel, "in any capacity where I can be of service to the Queen of our new world." It took Amica years to get used to being called Colonel; Queen, however, felt like an insult.

Amica didn't trust bringing the potential recruit to the base and had been planning a trip to visit their growing greenhouse sector in Leamington. The suspicious recruit was from a small town just prior called Chatham. She scheduled a visit with a promising prospect named Jerome in London, Ontario for a mid-morning meeting and a lunch with Alexia in Chatham, followed by a few greenhouse tours.

Arturo, Dawna, and Royelle decided to join her and added a Metal Fabrication shop in Chatham to their agenda. They wanted to speed up the filtration of the Great Lakes and were hoping to exchange the recycled metal they collected for a second filter for their hydro-powered watercraft. The filter had a massive six-by-ten-foot frame that was almost a foot thick. Every other day they had to remove the filter to clean it thoroughly. Two filters would keep things moving during cleaning.

The packed up a small army jeep with a few snacks, tumblers of water, some reusable bags, her emergency medical kit, rope, and a small shovel, as well as edible gifts Royelle made for the greenhouse growers. Amica also tucked her lucky jackknife into her shoulder bag. It contained a short knife, a corkscrew with a sharp point, a hard bottle-opener, and useless scissors. She started carrying it after Melanie died, realizing that self-defense was quite different than violence. It was a subject she intended on addressing with the committee.

Jerome was wonderful, respectful, and eager to help. He had several exciting crops to contribute, including a cannabis field, plus a watermelon, squash, and pumpkin patch. He also grew acres of both hot and sweet peppers. He was specifically interested in exchanging his crops for something different.

"I tossed out fields of watermelon and pumpkins last year because the people I trade with couldn't consume it all. There's another farmer with tomatoes and green beans, and one with two fields of corn. There's also a man on the other side of town who trades the fish he catches for cannabis and peppers, but he doesn't have enough fish to feed more than just us." His shoulders shrugged instinctually with his last statement.

B.E.S.T.

Jerome explained that the city had a few hundred people scattered about, most of whom traded services for food. London had quite a few businesses that still supplied companies in Toronto and money flowed more freely than the farming communities, however food was scarce.

Jerome was thrilled when the Colonel agreed to take a truck of their overages per week in exchange for six dozen of the protein bars Royelle made, three dozen of her berry purée spread, a dozen carrots, and three bottles of her homemade fruit juice, varying by season.

The team was feeling triumphant when they pulled into the last operational truckstop diner in all of Ontario to meet Alexia. The parking lot was full and there was a large sign at both the entrance and exit stating, "Cash preferred, supply trades accepted, and will feed in exchange for work." Miles of farm fields with long market stands were stretched out along its right side, and on the left side there was a gas station and car wash situated directly in front of a handmade furniture store.

"Wow, this is a thriving little community. Looks like they're already practicing the B.E.S.T. philosophies," Royelle commented once their vehicle was parked.

"Certainly appears so. Maybe Alexia can help us support each other's special version of utopia." Amica smiled, praying her earlier gut response was worrying over nothing.

"Did she pick this location, Colonel, or mention any ties to it?" Dawna asked.

"She picked it, but I didn't find any associated business or even individuals on social media. Anything in your search, Arturo?" Colonel Harrison responded.

"I found posts from 2036 when she worked at a chicken hatchery and shared several selfies showing a traditional rural lifestyle. There was only one current photo with her government web ID and it looked quite posh. I found no associations with anyone alarming," Her loyal assistant informed her as they walked into the outdated, yet noticeable clean restaurant.

They arrived over twenty minutes early and didn't expect Alexia to be waiting in a back booth. Her back was stiff like a board, eyes drilling into them and mouth emotionless. The hairs on Amica's neck stood at attention when their eyes connected overtop of the heads of random diner guests.

The Colonel cautiously approached, smiling and calm. With their eyes still focused on one another, she patted her chest, enlarging her smile in the same breath. Alexia mimicked the gesture, yet her face formed more of a smirk.

"Welcome to Chatham-Kent, Colonel." Alexia stood up, pushed her smile wider, and motioned for the trio to join her. The booth was two narrow for all five to sit, so Royelle and Amica sat across from Alexia, while Dawna and Arturo chose the adjacent table.

"Thank you for inviting us. I love this mini-city right here. Do you know who owns these businesses?" Colonel Harrison inquired.

"I thought you would appreciate this socialist gem. Everyone supports everyone. That's your plan, right?" Alexia's grin enlarged like the Cheshire Cat in the classic Alice in Wonderland.

"Doesn't that sound like a wonderful world to live in?" Royelle asked.

"It appears to be a true utopia of servitude. It is our duty to take care of those who cannot care for themselves. They will die if we do not share the resources required to live. That's why I took your survey. I know hard-working people who are ready to serve your dream, Queen Colonel." Alexia's cheeks remained pinned in their upright position.

"I am no queen, please, Alexia. It is not about serving me, it is about supporting one another and working together as a community," Colonel Harrison clarified.

"Yet, are these not your rules that we are being told to follow?" The obedience and blind acceptance she brazenly displayed initially was no longer masking her true thoughts.

"The rules were agreed upon by a committee, and anyone can raise concerns to a vote. It's not a governing body, more like agreed-upon guidelines to create a balanced, equitable, and stable society," The Colonel explained.

"Oh. Well, that would be good. There are considerable assets hidden here and we want a say in how they are used." Alexia's tight mouth began to relax.

"I can respect that. We have resources for trade; you can join the supplement meal program or you can keep your area running exactly the way it is right now. Our goal is to work together when needed, but still allow people to live life their own way. For example, if you have excess crops, we can swap them for something of ours that you would want. That's all we are trying to do." Alexia's intense stare softened as the Colonel spoke.

Amica continued, "If you don't need anything from us, the only thing we ask is that the community remains free from violence and guns. It looks like this area is already doing its part to contribute to the environment and economy."

"They would like to continue running this area and need fuel more than anything. It's our main cash source and spins this vicious cycle of us needing more cash to purchase gas. The restaurant mass-produces mini fruit and savory pies. They will gladly swap them for either gas or cash," Alexia advised.

"That could work. I have farmers in Leamington who send us vegetables in exchange for fruits and protein bars. I'm sure they will love homemade pies and would purchase them from you. I can work out a deal with their fuel supplier as well," The Colonel offered.

"Can I work with you on base camp and get more involved? I would like to help the community create a better world," Alexia asked

"Most definitely. I'm so glad you took that survey Alexia. I believe you will be a genuine asset to B.E.S.T." The Colonel accepted her offer eagerly.

Amica realized the young lady's original answers came off as forced and fake because she had her own doubts and her responses were not sincere. Alexia's shoulders dropped from their perched position now that Amica demonstrated their utopia was a partnership rather than a dictatorship. Her defenses were down and her interest revealed itself to be genuine.

Alexia agreed to stay in Chatham long enough to facilitate the first resource exchange and then she would meet the team back at the base in Trenton. The recruitment team left Chatham and headed the short drive to Leamington to visit the greenhouses.

Operations were robust and expanding. The Colonel gave them each one hundred thousand dollars more from the funds collected during the Australian ship sales, four dozen jars of blueberry preserves, six dozen blueberry tarts, and two hundred protein bars. In exchange, the greenhouses were sending four truckloads stuffed with cannabis, lettuce, green peppers, tomatoes, mini cucumbers, and corn.

The team drove back to Trenton as the sun began to set, celebrating how their nugget of hope had grown into a global effort to save the world. Faith in humanity and the power of teamwork was all anyone really needed to survive, and it was blooming everywhere.

Back on Solid Ground

Back on the base, Amica began her morning with her usual running route towards the now almost leafless twisted tree. The air nipped at her neck, chilling the sweat that she collected while picking up speed during the last downward slope. Sparkling drops of dew that scattered in the tall grass caught her eye, and she slowed down.

The tiny, glass-like beads danced off the rising sun, shimmering with potential and promise. Peace would be possible. The Colonel felt a long-forgotten calmness in the air as she circled the tree and headed back to her team.

Colonel Harrison kept in close contact with Captain John and was relieved to receive the wrist alert update that the team was preparing to dock in Vancouver, unharmed and victorious. Amica sent their only carrier plane to escort them back to the base, where everyone else continued preparing for their arrival.

Amica asked Royelle, Kali, Mei, Tobin, and Arturo to put together an elaborate feast to welcome home the crew. They went above and beyond, even securing a rare treat from Commander Ying's last trip to the remains of South Korea, salted cod and flash-frozen catfish. They made rice patties and wheat bread from Australia's last harvest, and grilled lobsters from the East Coast. The bar was stocked with local wine and craft beer that Calvin and Ariel had secured on one of their excursions in exchange for some of their cannabis crop.

Dawna, Calvin, Ariel, and David spruced up sixteen houses located close to the base, so everyone on the ship had their own space to sleep once they returned. They filled their fridges with fresh fruits and sweets. They left a bottle of daily supplements and a sleep mask by their bed. They placed fragrant hygiene kits and bath bombs next to the sinks in each washroom.

The Colonel and every founding member of B.E.S.T. understood the time they sacrificed and the risk they took being on that ship. Her instructions were to make sure every single member of that team felt like heroes and knew how grateful they were for their service.

"Every member of B.E.S.T. is a critical part of our success, but for the next week or so, I want these sixteen to really feel extra-appreciated. Some of the most selfish and dangerous people left on this planet are now trapped far away, giving us a safer opportunity to rebuild a kind, equitable world.

"It wouldn't be possible without the crew that should be pulling in at any moment. Let's greet them with the loudest cheer you can muster; spread out six feet apart, spanning the entire base." The Colonel was standing on the steps of the mess hall high enough to see the crowd of hundreds who gathered to celebrate their return.

When the team finally showed up several minutes later, everyone whistled and cheered, the roar lasting longer than the time it took to unboard the team and their belongings. The enthusiastic reunion of well wishes, salutes, handshakes, and hugs for those wearing masks carried on until the group made their way to where the Colonel was standing.

That's when Amica noticed there was an unfamiliar face in the crowd. In every discussion that took place between the Colonel and Captain John, there was no mention of picking up any additional passengers. All eyes were on her and the crew, so she shook it off and proceeded almost as planned.

"Welcome back, everyone, and I guess welcome as well for the guest whom you picked up along the way. Hello, sir. We are so grateful that this extraordinary group of sixteen heroes risked themselves while sacrificing time and comfort for the greater good of B.E.S.T. We've prepared a feast inside to celebrate your successful mission and to welcome you back into our now thriving community," Amica graciously greeted each one with a direct look in the eye, accompanied by a slow nod of her head.

She stared exceptionally hard at the unfamiliar face and then again at the man who failed to inform her of the extra body. The Colonel felt bad that accommodations and gifts hadn't been arranged for him like the other crew members, then was perplexed as to where they could have found him along their journey. The plane was waiting for them when they arrived in Vancouver and it was a non-stop flight to the base. Her mind raced with wonder.

"Please, everyone, go inside, eat until your hearts are content, and soak in the appreciation of your teammates. We have private housing available for when you're ready for some rest on solid ground." She motioned towards the door to the canteen before adding, "Captain John, may we chat for a moment."

"Yes, of course," He answered, obviously anticipating the Colonel's pending questions.

"May I join your chat, Colonel Harrison? I think I may be solely responsible for its subject matter," Tamika politely interjected.

"Welcome back to both of you. Thank you for your service. Now Tamika, did you invite our new guest?" Amica turns to face her.

"Yes, but with very good reasons and what I feel is sound judgment. I trust you will agree he is not a threat and deserves to be here," Tamika stated without hesitation.

"I doubt you'd make a rash decision that could jeopardize us; I have faith in you. Who is he and where did you find him?" The Colonel inquired, praying he wasn't one of the men they just robbed for a doomsdays trip to a deserted island.

"His name is William. He was a passenger on the ship." The Colonel couldn't hide her gasp as that same fear had just entered her mind. Tamika continued unfettered, "He was not like the others. He showed compassion and wants to work to repair our earth. He thought Australia was a way to escape the violence."

"Are you certain his intentions are pure? Why would he choose the ship over signing B.E.S.T.'s contract?" Although it was her intent to trust Tamika, Amica couldn't restrain her doubts.

"William was tired of having to fight to survive and didn't think B.E.S.T. offered any protection. He thought he could build a better world in Australia. He is now willing to sign and will help us revive the land. I believe him to be trustworthy, and take full responsibility for ensuring that he is not a threat," Tamika assured the Colonel.

"I see. I can admit it is possible. I knew my plan to segregate based on the misinformation campaign had a margin of error. If he is a good man and you saved him from whatever horrific fate awaits in Australia, then you saved my soul, as well as his. Thank you, Tamika." Colonel Harrison was wise enough to know her judgment wasn't flawless and feared sending someone good to a place destined for utter destruction.

"Thank you, Colonel. My gut has a good feeling about him. He took good care of me on the ship and will care for our country the same." Tamika extended her hand, which Amica gently squeezed in return.

"I hope so, now let's join the festivities!" The Colonel's enthusiasm was renewed and they headed the hall together with Captain John, and poor William, who was pacing aimlessly a few feet away throughout their conversation.

Ever since there was a rise in contagious virus pandemics, dining together had taken a different form. Without hesitating, each person pulled out their mask, with the noticeable exception of William. He halted in his tracks, took two steps back, and couldn't apologize fast enough.

"I'm so sorry, I don't have a mask. I knew that was a polite practice in Canada during the pandemics, but it was never really embraced when I was living down south the last few years. I can wait outside. I don't mind," He sputtered while cursing himself loudly in his head. He wanted to fit in, proof he was a willing teammate, and so far it was off to a rocky start.

"Do not worry. I have new ones still in their packaging." Captain John pulled one out of his travel sack and handed a bright blue mask to William.

"Thank you. I appreciate it." He graciously accepted it and eagerly put it on.

The canteen had a long banquet table along the entrance with well over one hundred one-foot-by-one-foot, four-inch-high metal boxes. Each person picked up their box and found a seat in the modern cafeteria-style setting. To prevent the spread of germs, each rectangular table consisted of ten chairs with a tic tac board-style plexiglass divider blocking off each person's dining area. The glass was two and a half feet high, but thin enough that you could hear those closest to you.

The inside of the box had two layers, a thin area with a metal plate, and utensils. When the divider was slid aside, it revealed a warm cheese and chive wheat bun, a hard boiled egg on top of a warm spinach, pumpkin seed and ricotta salad, a three-cheese rice patty, and a fish stew topped with a piece of lobster. A separate dish contained a large scoop of apple crumble.

Calvin and Ariel scored four bricks of cheddar cheese, two bricks of mozzarella, and four buckets of ricotta from a dairy farmer who exchanged it for cash and security. Someone stole a cow from his property one week, and then the following week, someone else (possibly the same someone) drained his silos in the middle of the night.

Calvin produced enough seventeen-foot walls out of recyclables to protect the farmer's property and gave him two hundred dollars (with the Colonel's blessing) to keep him afloat until he was able to produce more milk to sell at the local markets.

Now that they were no longer assigned to building wall material, Calvin and Ariel spent their days on the hunt for resources, occasionally sneaking off for a private, sometime public, romantic rendezvous. Most memorable was their trip after they brought home the cheese; still high from their earlier win, they couldn't contain themselves when they found an abandoned grocery store that no one had looted.

"Holy shitballs, Cal! There has to be almost fifty bags of noodles, still edible. Cans of tomatoes, potatoes, beans, corn, and even pasta sauce! We won't be able to fit it all on one trip," Ariel shouted, dancing through the aisles.

"There's no rush to load it. We have this entire place to ourselves, let's dance." He scooped her into his arms, and they waltzed past long expired boxes of cereal and granola.

"You make me happy. Seriously happy," Ariel whispered in his ear.

"I've never felt this good in my life and I know that has everything to do with you." He stopped long enough to look her in the eye, emphasizing each word slowly.

A passionate kiss, turned into rubbing up against each other's bodies, gently, then more frantically. Pushing their weight into one another, as if to meld into one. Calvin's hands glided along her tiny bum, before darting around her thighs until it reached the spot aching for his touch. She pressed her body into his, until there was no light between them. Not a word was spoken as they both slid out of their clothes and into one another.

The ceiling-high front windows exposed them to the empty street, but the fear of someone possibly discovering their naked explosion wasn't even a fleeting thought. Their eager instruments made extraordinary music together and they wanted the world to hear.

Calvin's mind replayed the experience over and over as he stared at her through the plexiglass inside the canteen hall. The silly divider was only a temporary separation for the sake of society. He was certain he'd be that close to Ariel again, really soon, as he fantasized about their previous times together.

Calvin was content with the shared meal and bountiful harvest they were given, especially knowing the hand he had in procuring so many of the ingredients. The people around felt more and more like family, and he could no longer imagine life without Ariel, or the rest of the team in the B.E.S.T. community. He was grinning gleefully when the Colonel's voice rose within the large space.

"Hello, everyone. Thank you for being here. I hope you're enjoying the meal our chefs have prepared." A sincere cheer rose in the crowd, prompting the Colonel to pause for a few seconds. "It's the best thing I've eaten in years! How many other people missed cheese?"

A roar of applause filled the massive room.

"I can't possibly thank everyone individually who helped secure, prepare, and deliver the food for us tonight, not without including the farmers who grew it, the laborers who processed it, and the community that has taken teamwork to a whole new level. Every team member within the B.E.S.T. community and everyone on that ship, thank you. Thank you!" Her sincerity was unmistakable.

"Every person who made tonight's event possible, thank you. Each and every one of you believed in my plan and have worked so hard to make it a reality, I am grateful to you." Tears weighed on the delicate bags underneath her eyes, tempting to overflow uncontrollably. Her gratitude poured from her face.

Emotions took the best of the stoic Colonel and she sat down before finishing her planned introduction; fortunately Kali was ready and waiting. "Thank you, Colonel, for creating an environment where we can thrive! I haven't felt this safe and happy since I was a little girl playing board games with my family."

Heads bobbed in agreement, so Kali continued. "My family and friends created a nine-person game, like volleyball, during one of Canada's pandemic lockdowns. I think we can turn it into a forty-five-person game, even one hundred and eighty, since the more people involved just means it will last longer and we should have more balls up in the air.

"When everyone is done eating, please meet me outside on the old training grounds if you want to play. We've marked off three-foot-by-three-foot segments in the back field for crop planting in the Spring, but we can use it since there is nothing in the ground yet." Kali had mentioned the game to a few people prior to today's celebration who couldn't wait to try it.

Organized sports and group activities were sorely missed; everyone eagerly inhaled the last bites of their meal, cleaned up their areas and rushed outside. No one knew exactly what she had in mind, but eighty-six people made their way to the field and picked a square. Many others found a spot around the perimeter to watch. Once everyone was situated either in a game spot or on the sidelines, Kali began explaining the rules through a virtual wrist presentation she had prepared prior.

"The object of the game is to keep the ball in the air. If it lands on the ground, the last one to touch it has to sit on the ground and can no longer play, creating a weak spot within the larger square. You are not allowed to step outside of your square and you can use any part of your body to keep the ball in the air, as long as the ball doesn't touch the ground. The last person standing is the winner! Since we have eighty-six people, we will start with six volleyballs in the air. Who wants one?" The leggy brunette opened up a netted bag and lifted the first ball above her head.

Hands shot up, some enthusiastically, some with reverence, and others who pulled theirs down just as quickly in regret. Kali tossed out six balls and let them land where they may. "Okay, hold the balls until the count of three and then send them up high to the sky. If it hits the ground, you've got to sit down!"

Silliness and laughter ensued, making Kali, the Colonel, and everyone in attendance feel good about the future. They worked hard for months and truly deserved to enjoy a chance to reward themselves.

Every Life Lost

The crew returned from Australia unharmed and word quickly spread of the people who B.E.S.T. had tricked into relocating onto a sinking, barren Australia. A few riots and protests exploded in the old New United Republic, demanding someone rescue those who were left to die. Of course, no one made any attempt to do so, and the concern died down as fast as it rose.

All satellite towers, wireless connections, and internet service providers were destroyed prior to the ship arriving. As far as the Colonel was aware, no one heard anything directly from those in the Badlands of Australia. There was no method for the defrauded to tell the masses how they willingly paid for their own death sentence.

B.E.S.T. was living up to its name in most regards, though it was certainly not without its flaws. People occasionally ratted out their neighbors for breaking the rules, and the pettiness of some complaints made it impossible to kick everyone out who wasn't in full compliance.

The most common infractions were not growing a tree or being caught smoking tobacco. The Colonel was familiar with the fierce hold of having an addiction and announced that with the exception of the first rule to remain non-violent, they would allow a ninety-day grace period for each member from the date they first joined.

Amica was accommodating, accepting, almost apologetic, when someone would go against the vision she had for their new world. At the welcome home ceremony, when Tamika explained who William was to her, Amica realized that more men and women like him could have been left to die. William was wonderful, and it was perfectly possible that other decent human beings chose the same fatal path. The passengers weren't given the chance to understand exactly what they were choosing.

Wars were escalating on the other side of the wall. The Colonel didn't want to sacrifice another life unless she had no other choice. She encouraged every member to keep their distance from the border wall. In her optimistic mind, she could keep everyone safe as long as there was a wall dividing the two opposing worlds.

Unfortunately, a little more than five months after the wall was finished, two residents of B.E.S.T. would no longer be safe within those walls. One to later be expelled permanently, and another soul murdered under her watch.

Royelle, Gia, Kali, Dawna, Josée, Tamika, and Kristie were having a celebratory iced tea cocktail with Amica that she made using an eighteen-year-old bottle of tequila. Amica had been carrying around the birthday gift from her ex for years, hoping to find a reason to celebrate. They were just finishing their first glass when Arturo interrupted their loud laughter with the urgent message.

There was an escalating domestic assault happening in Markham. A woman was being held by a man with a gun who was threatening to shoot her or anyone else who came close. Law enforcement was no longer paid and therefore unavailable, so the Colonel's military expertise was called in to diffuse the situation.

Each of her evening guests insisted on going with her, and Arturo was admandent he wouldn't leave her side. The Colonel didn't want a crowd to overwhelm the situation. It was one man with one gun; no need to put any additional lives in jeopardy if it wasn't necessary.

"Josée and Tamika, you have already risked your lives and sacrificed so much. I'd prefer you sit this one out. I don't want to scare the gunman with a big group, so we'll take two POP duets. Royelle and I can take one, as I always need her for moral support. I'd like Dr. Romano to come along in case we need medical help, and Arturo, who is skilled in martials arts in case we need some fancy footwork." Colonel Harrison gave a cute wink in her assistant's direction, wrapping up her quick decision before motioning for the three who were going to make their way outside.

When they arrived on scene, the woman was already dead, and the person who called in the disturbance was hiding inside an old bank vestibule. They parked their cars around the corner, messaging the individual inside to unlock the door once they arrived.

"It's only about twenty feet, so run like your life depends on it. I'll go first and hold the door open," The Colonel directed her three colleagues.

"What can we do to help once we're inside?" Dr. Romano asked.

"Good question. I was hoping she would still be alive and I could negotiate with him. I'm open to suggestions." Colonel Harrison didn't have a viable weapon or any leverage. Arturo had a bag with rope, tape, and a knife, none of which could compete with a gun.

"We need to create a distraction in front, while someone grabs him from behind." Royelle was already envisioning the takedown, and as a surprise to even herself, she wanted to be the one to tackle him.

"That could work. We could make a racket from inside the bank; the glass should be bulletproof." The gears in the Colonel's head began to turn. "The front door to the building behind him is open. I'll go around the block; hopefully there's a back door I can go in."

"Can I go, Amica?" The words surprised Royelle's lips as they burst free from between them.

"Are you sure? It's very risky. He could hear you approach and shoot you without any warning." The Colonel was now shaking with the nerves of something happening to her lifelong friend.

"Yes, I am. If you make enough noise in front, I can sneak up behind him. I've watched you be brave for years. It's my turn. I need to do this for my own self-worth." Royelle's face displayed the seriousness of her request.

"You've always been a hero to me, but you can do this if you're sure about it." Colonel Harri's voice cracked mid-sentence.

"I am sure. You can count on me." Her words were as firm as her gaze.

"I always have. Alright, let's put the plan into motion. Arturo, can you give her the rope and knife?" Amica rallied.

"Got it, Colonel." Arturo pulled out the supplies and handed it to Royelle.

The remaining three agreed to wait until Royelle was in position, hidden safely behind the shooter, before they would make their move towards the bank. Just before Royelle scurried off, Amica gave her a super big squeeze and they exchanged sincere I-love-you-s.

Royelle ran across the street, around the block, and was out of sight before the gunman even glanced in their direction. The Colonel's wrist alert went off and the words "READY" appeared only a few minutes later. Amica repeated her earlier instructions and asked the caller inside the vestibule to be prepared to unlock the door in a matter of seconds. The threesome bolted from their hiding spot and booked it to the bank.

Colonel Harrison grabbed the glass door, but it was still locked. She knocked lightly, and it took a few seconds for the person inside to get close enough to open it before immediately running back inside to hide behind a large filing cabinet. Amica held it open wide for Gia and Arturo to dart inside, and just as she was about to follow, she heard a snap and felt a force penetrate through her upper arm.

Colonel Harrison fell forward, half-inside the door. Arturo scooped her up, carrying her out of sight. Instantaneously, Royelle heard the shot, and peeked out to witness the dark red blood fly from her dear friend's body. A power she had never felt before filled her own slender figure, pushing her out from behind the door frame. Not giving the shooter a chance to react, Royelle jumped on top of the man, knocking his gun down the stairs.

Dr. Romano tended to Amica's arm, and Arturo turned back towards the shooter just as Royelle was laying him out flat. Arturo called back to the ladies that Royelle had been successful and he'd return to assist the Colonel.

"Go help Royelle keep him secure," Amica said between labored breaths.

"The Colonel will be fine," Doctor Romano assured her worried assistant.

Arturo nodded in agreement and went outside to help his other friend, Royelle. As he was climbing up the concrete stairs, he saw Royelle swinging punches at the back of the man's head, blood and saliva flying everywhere.

Arturo raced towards them, securing the gun as he passed by it. The man was unconscious. Royelle let go and exhaled loudly. The pair shared an exasperated stare before she stood up and took a step back. Arturo wrapped the man's wrists in the rope she had dropped when she jumped on top of him. Neither spoke as the man laid motionless on the cracked cement. Adrenaline had taken over, and Royelle was still in fight-or-flight mode.

She physically shook off the weight of what had just happened and took off running towards Amica. Arturo double-checked the man's throat for a pulse, faint but still there. He sighed deeply, fearing his friend might have just killed a man in a moment of blind rage. Arturo turned the gunman over on his back and propped him up. The sweaty man had a bushy beard, sticky with fresh blood and spit. The drip from his nose had slowed and his eyes fluttered, trying to regain their sight. His body began to stir.

Arturo's military training taught him never to give an enemy an opportunity to escape. The trained soldier tied an extra rope around the man's ankles, and hog-tied it to the ropes around his wrist. He still had a kevlar spring coil in his bag, which he looped through the thickest part of where the ankle met his wrists, whipped him onto his back, and tied the Kevlar coil to a metal porch railing.

"Amica! Are you alright?" Royelle hollered as she swung open the entrance door to the bank.

The Colonel was sitting upright with her left arm and shoulder wrapped up tightly. She smiled, giving her forever friend a second to pause long enough to do the same.

"I saw the blood and thought the worst." Tears ran down Royelle's cheeks as she wheezed each word out between the tears.

"I get knocked down, but I get back up again." Her confidence was beaming brightly as always.

"I should have known you'd be fine," Royelle said, shaking her head slowly.

"What happened to the gunman?" Amica asked, just as Arturo walked in.

"I don't know. Ask him. My emotions took over and everything was a blur." Royelle's heart was racing too fast from adrenaline to think straight.

"I believe he is no longer a threat. In her efforts to detain him, Royelle hurt him pretty bad. I'm not sure if there's brain damage or any permanent effects. He was trying to get out from under her, so she was pounding on him to stay down. He's tied up and quite secure at the moment." Arturo created his own explanation for the violent rage he witnessed minutes prior.

"I wasn't trying to kill him," Royelle pleaded at Arturo.

"I know that was not your intent, and do believe he will live," Arturo answered quickly.

"I went a little nutty, Amica. I was afraid he'd overpower me if I didn't knock him unconscious," Royelle continued.

"I understand. We'll figure this out. Don't worry, my friend," Colonel Harrison assured her.

"I'll go with Arturo to check on the gunman while you rest a little longer, Amica. I want to make sure it clots," Gia suggested.

"Thank you, Dr. Romano. I appreciate you." The Colonel's breathing was still erratic and her words didn't have their usual command. Although the bullet created a clean exit and entry wound and it was far from life threatening, the pain was intense. Royelle slid into a spot on the floor next to Amica, leaning her head on her uninjured shoulder. Amica squeezed her hand and the pair rested in silence until Arturo and Gia returned with their new prisoner.

Crystal-Clear Waters

Dawna had been waiting all night to make a big announcement when the Colonel's domestic violence emergency killed the mood. Their filtration system had passed through all five lakes enough times that they were excelling far beyond expectations in their chemical testing. It was not only non-toxic, it was clean enough that you could safely drink from it after going through a simple filter and boiling process.

Life within the lake was flourishing, and to prove it, varieties of fish were thriving. Dawna needed visual evidence to share with Amica, and Kali had suggested taking underwater videos. The test results were impressive, but seeing the crystal-clear quality of the water was what blew both women away.

After a second day of passing the device through Lake Michigan and pulling out virtually empty filters, they decided it was safe to go back into the water. Dawna was the first one brave enough to put her feet in, walking outwards until she was up to her knees, astonished she could still see her toe nails. Kali followed at twice the speed, letting joyous giggles escape with each step further into the sand and earth beneath.

A couple of weeks before the Colonel invited them for celebratory drinks at her place, both women put on a swimsuit and used a subscope visual recorder (SVR) to capture everything beneath the surface of the lakes they cleaned. SVRs were underwater goggles connected to their eye muscles using sensors, so they could video tape exactly what the women saw. The frame of the lenses shone an LED beam that illuminated every detail, capturing the scene with surreal clarity.

Creative whiz Kali spliced the most vivid and brilliant clips from their swim together, adding text bubbles and arrows pointing out the diversity in the lake and triumphant horns to the end while the caption, "The future looks crystal clear" flashed across the screen.

The underwater video showcased more species of fish and plant life than either woman could successfully identify. It took Dawna's breath away, and she was waiting for a break in the conversation to explain the exciting news before sharing the link via their wristbands. Everyone was rambling with stories from the last few months, as it was their first opportunity to sit down, relax, and connect again.

B.E.S.T.

When Arturo crashed the party with the news of a gunman, the Colonel's remaining guests finished their drinks and went home for the night. Once the foursome returned from their mission, the death of one woman, the gunshot taken by their leader, and Royelle being under scrutiny for using violence overwhelmed the residents of B.E.S.T. with worry and stress.

The leaders were frantically establishing fair rules for a virtual trial and a method that would allow every active member of B.E.S.T. to watch and vote on the outcome. Thanks to instant online polling, a jury of his peers would actually consist of any of his peers who cared enough to participate.

Still wanting to share the good news without taking focus on the biggest issues, Dawna chose to send a blue alert through her band to only the Colonel, merely stating, "Progress in the Great Lakes has been quite positive and we're ready to move onto other bodies of water. Please watch the video via the link, which will showcase how beautifully our underwater world is thriving."

The video of Lake Michigan, Lake Ontario, and Lake Huron was taken over the course of a week and compiled together into a musical snapshot of vibrant color and underwater movement. Only twenty minutes after she sent Amica the eighteen minute video, the Colonel responded,

"This is incredible! Dawna, you continue to amaze me. Thank you. Please keep doing what you're doing anywhere you can. Much appreciated, Colonel Amica Harrison."

Dawna was grinning with pride, which exploded moments later when she received a second alert that her video had been distributed by the Colonel through the entire B.E.S.T. network, captioned with, "B.E.S.T. is blessed with Dawna Marchand, Kali Robbins, Doctor Romano, Doctor Sinclair, Calvin Kilne, and the entire team who transformed our Great Lakes back into the tranquil beauty you're about to see!"

Prosecuted By Projection

Harvard Lewis was the name of the gunman who committed the first murder within the B.E.S.T. membership and they needed him to live. If he died, an investigation into the cause of his death would have been required and could have ended very badly for Royelle.

As lifelong friends who shared unfiltered dialogue without giving it a second thought, they discussed his fate frankly, focused on what outcome was the most preferable, while waiting for their prisoner to wake up.

"If he dies, I will be expelled for murder," Royelle insisted.

"No, you won't; it was self-defense. I think I've found a way for us to work past that challenge. If he lives and is expelled, we'll have a dangerous enemy lurking on the other side, waiting for revenge." Amica was quickly pacing the one-by-eighteen-foot- wide strip of flooring behind her office desk as she spoke.

"So, you'd prefer he'd die." Royelle raised her eyebrow, not believing her friend would be so callous.

"At least that would be God's call instead of mine. What if we take the pressure off both of us and put these decisions to a vote? If he lives, we have a trial to discuss the facts and air it virtually. Then we can take an ISAP (Instant Signal Alert Poll) and go with the majority," Amica spit out the idea with a sense of relief.

"Will you have to put me on trial?" Royelle couldn't look her in the eyes as she asked.

"We can take that decision to a vote as well. After the trial, we could do a separate ISAP asking if they believe your actions were in the best interest of B.E.S.T." The thought of risking her friend's future to strangers terrified her, yet she knew that was the only way to be unbiased.

"What if they kick me out?" Royelle couldn't envision life on the other side.

"I doubt they will, considering he had just taken a shot at me and all our lives were in obvious danger. Prior to the trial, I'll propose an amendment to our first rule. It should read, 'Anyone who initiates violence of any kind will result in immediate expulsion from B.E.ST.

However, defending yourself against an attack is justifiable,' at least in my opinion," Amica suggested.

"If you're taking it to a vote, I hope everyone else thinks like you," Royelle said nervously.

"We'll figure this out together. You've always had extraordinary faith in me; don't lose it now," Amica pleaded to her bestie with each word.

Royelle gave a slow nod as Amica leaned over to tightly squeeze her friend. They didn't exchange another word. Royelle wandered off in one direction pondering what all of this meant while Amica went back into her office to lay out the groundwork for an upcoming trial.

Colonel Harrison fussed over every detail, even the method in which the crimes would be categorized, in the assumption that future trials would be required. Using the defendant's initials, the individual's number of offenses on record, and the term and condition that were broken, she came up with HL2-1/2 to reference how Harvard Lewis would be charged with two accounts, breaking the first and second condition of B.E.S.T. membership.

She reread the alert notifying every member of an upcoming trial twelve times before finally clicking send. The lifelong atheist whispered to an unknown deity, "Protect Royelle. Give us true justice," as her intentions were announced to the community.

B.E.S.T. TRIAL NOTICE: HL2-1/2

As a community we will review the events of April nineteenth, 2042 that led to the murder of Elizabeth Lewis and gunshot wound of Colonel Amica Harrison to determine if Harvard Lewis should be expelled from B.E.S.T. for breaking the first two conditions of our community. In the event Harvard Lewis does not survive and is unable to attend his own trial, we will expand the trial scope to include the actions that led to his demise.

Any witnesses can register in advance to share their first-hand testimony. Harvard Lewis will be given a chance to speak on his own behalf once he is well enough to do so. The trial will be shared through your projection bands and everyone can vote instantly upon completion. You will be asked whether Harvard Lewis should remain in B.E.S.T. and if anyone else's actions on April nineteenth, 2042 should be reviewed more closely.

Please review the attached amendment to our first rule and vote on this ISAP if you'd like to proceed with this change: 'Anyone who initiates violence of any kind will result in immediate expulsion from B.E.ST. However, defending yourself against an attack is justifiable."

Stay safe, sincerely, Colonel Harrison

* * *

Once again, one click of Amica's wrist sent a plan into motion where the uncontrolled variables made her nauseous. It was a tad easier each time, but the specific consequences of events not going as she hoped kept her mind racing. Harvard must be expelled and Royelle's violence during his arrest had to be deemed justified. Her conscience couldn't accept any other outcome; if she believed it to be so, it would be so.

The read rate and acceptance response on the trial alert far exceeded past communication. In less than ten minutes of hitting the network, eighty-eight percent of the B.E.S.T. membership registered to watch and participate in the virtual trial HL2-1/2. By the end of the day, it surpassed ninety-five percent, representing millions of diverse individuals who would tune in and vote. The amendment to the first rule passed with a vote of fifty-seven thousand, eight hundred and nineteen to only one hundred and sixty-four objections. A great sigh was released from deep within Amica when Harvard woke up less than an hour later.

Colonel Harrison, Arturo, Doctor Gia Romano, and Royelle signed up as witnesses, as well as Patrick Burns, the person who first reported the shooting. Another young woman who watched everything from her window registered the following day and a nurse from the hospital where Harvard was taken after the shooting offered her expertise for the trial. A former Provincial Court of Appeals judge volunteered to be available for any legal definitions or explanations that pertained to their case.

They mapped out a detailed timeline of the events leading up to his arrest and how Royelle chose to subdue a man far greater in physical size. When Arturo described the sight he walked in on, after Harvard was on the ground, it made Royelle shrink.

"The truth will set you free, my friend," Amica offered instinctually.

"But first it will piss you off." Royelle tried to sound angry, but appreciative of her friend's best intentions. She cracked a smile before the sentence was complete.

"True dat!" The Colonel kept the mood as light as she could, knowing Royelle's aggressive actions had been the result of fear: a fear Harvard initiated.

When the trial approached, every witness was asked to be segregated in their own quarters for their testimony and question period. Each witness would be given up to sixty minutes to describe what they saw in as much detail as possible, followed by a thirty-minute public question period. Anyone could submit a question during the hour testimonial, which the witness would be required to answer by the end of their time slot.

The trial would begin with the Colonel explaining the process and sharing the timeline with the virtual courtroom. The first hour was dedicated to Harvard explaining his side of the story. During his testimonial, he bounced between lies and excuses, never settling on one clear defense strategy.

"I am not a violent man. I was driven to violence and then viciously attacked when I was merely defending myself. I am an innocent man that got jumped from behind and then beat down like a dog. No chance to explain myself, just violently attacked. I am the victim." Harvard's leathery skin glistened with sweat beads as he attempted to restrain himself from shouting.

"All of these women punched me repeatedly: my wife, the Colonel's soldiers. It was that one blonde woman who caused me to shoot the Colonel. They're trying to cover up their brutality; it's all lies. My wife attacked me and I shot her in self-defense. She had a knife. She hit me and I thought she would stab me. A man has a right to protect himself, even if it is from a woman." Harvard's arms were secured to the armrest of his chair, causing him to buck his body forward wildly whenever he'd instinctively go to use his hands to emphasize his anger.

"Now I'm scared, in shock over what happened, and some woman lunges at me, causing my gun to go off. I wasn't aiming at the Colonel. I'm a skilled shooter. I would have struck her dead in the temple if I intended the bullet for her. I am telling you that I am the victim! It was an elaborate set-up from the beginning that my wife cooked up," He screamed into the camera.

Harvard continued ranting various scenarios for forty minutes, before surrendering his remaining time. "You're going to toss me out whatever I do, because everyone believes women over men. Don't fall for their trap. They are not as innocent as they claim to be! Sure, but go ahead, kick me out of this crackpot place. I'm done justifying self-defense to bleeding-heart feminists."

A series of questions were posted in the chat, ranging from:

What happened to the knife after your wife was killed?

Why was the gun pointed at the Colonel when Royelle attacked you?

Why do you own a gun when it's against B.E.S.T. rules?

Harvard read each question and answered them with two words, "Fuck you."

The Colonel expected Harvard to be more convincing, but his inability to keep the story straight and his unwillingness to answer questions made Amica feel considerably better about the pending outcome.

Colonel Harrison was the next one to provide her testimony, starting with the call she received about the incident. "As you will hear from the remaining witnesses, I received a call from Patrick Burns on April nineteenth, 2042 because a woman was being held hostage. Patrick saw Harvard with a gun pointed at his now-deceased wife's head. Arturo, Royelle, and Dr. Gia Romano went with me to help diffuse the situation. When we arrived, it was already too late."

Amica answered every question honestly, providing as much detail as she could without expressing her opinion on the matter. It was essential to her effectiveness as a leader that the body of members watching knew that she was a woman of integrity.

The Colonel's testimony was followed by Patrick Burns, Arturo, and Dr. Romano confirming the same timeline and description of events. The woman who watched from the window emphasized that she did not see Harvard's wife with a knife. Royelle was the last person to speak before Harvard would be given a final chance to defend himself prior to the B.E.S.T. community vote. She turned her camera and microphone on, and then froze. Fear overwhelmed her.

B.E.S.T.

The Colonel had already switched the conference presenter to Royelle and all eyes were on her, patiently waiting for her to begin. Silence lingered for seconds that stretched into minutes. Tears trickled down Royelle's cheeks as her rapid short breaths echoed across every member's virtual screens. Amica knew she wasn't supposed to intervene, but her heart superseded her head.

"Royelle, take a moment, get a sip of water, and we will break for ten minutes. I'm sure we're all due for a bio break," The Colonel announced into the virtual crowd. She turned off the presentation screen for Royelle and replaced it with her favorite meme showing a woman squeezing her legs together outside a public restroom, "Take a break, before URINE in trouble."

Then she sent a private alert to Royelle with a hug emoji and the words, *You can do this.* When the break was over, Colonel Harrison went straight to Royelle's testimony, who found the strength to spit everything out in a clear, concise way in spite of its speed.

"I never intended to hurt Harvard Lewis. Colonel Harrison received the call about the hostage situation, just as she described. I went along to support her in what I assumed would be a hostage negotiation. I had no intention of getting involved or harming anyone." Royelle exhaled and continued her rehearsed retelling of the events.

"When we arrived, Harvard's wife was already lying on the sidewalk, lifeless. You could see the pool of blood, and he was firing random shots in the area. We assessed the situation and agreed that trying to talk to him would be a suicide mission. We needed a distraction and someone to tackle him." Royelle started off talking as fast as her heart was racing, but felt calmer with each word.

"I ended up volunteering; in fact, I insisted on it. I was partially worried that he would peg me off if I chose to run to the vestibule, as I'm most likely the slowest of the four. My arms are quite strong, I have the height leverage, and took self-defense when I was younger. Something told me this was my time to step up for the Colonel and for every member of B.E.S.T.

"The Colonel, Arturo, and Dr. Romano waited for me to hide inside the building directly behind the gunman and then took off running towards the bank. I snuck out slowly, and that's when I saw

Harvard fire directly at my friends without giving any warning. I witnessed the blood splatter and saw the Colonel fall over.

"My instincts must have kicked in, or maybe anger over him shooting my friend, but I jumped on him without hesitation. He was trying to fight back, and bucking from beneath me. I pushed all my force into him to keep him down. I did hit him from behind when I was on top of him. I promise I was trying to detain him, not cause greater physical injury."

Royelle had more questions than anyone else when she finished speaking, but she answered each with certainty and confidence. Even the person who asked whether she enjoyed smashing the murderer's head into the ground received an honest and compassionate response: "No, most definitely not. I was scared he would overpower me. I felt nauseous when I saw the blood. I've never hurt anyone and was unaware of my strength."

Once the questions for Royelle ceased, Harvard was giving one last chance to appeal to masses.

"That whore lies. She tackled me, the gun went off, and then she was bashing my head into the ground over and over. I blacked out and couldn't fight back. I have permanent brain damage thanks to that crazy bitch," Harvard began shouting into the screen the moment it was his turn again.

The Colonel let him rant for ten minutes before his swearing became a substitute for every second word. He wasn't providing any new testimonial or giving any honest answers, and it was time to vote on the outcome.

"Unless anyone has any final questions for Harvard, I believe the facts of the case have been described in full. Harvard Lewis has been given ample opportunity to plead his case and it is your decision if the murder of his wife and assault on the Colonel is reason enough to expel Harvard permanently from the B.E.S.T. community.

"It doesn't appear any questions have been posted. Everyone who was logged in for the trial has sixty minutes to cast their vote. There will be two polls as you exit the meeting; the first is a yes or no question asking if Harvard Lewis is guilty of inciting violence. A yes vote will remove him from our borders.

"The next question is whether the charge of violence was committed by any other member of B.E.S.T. during the arrest. If you feel the response was warranted even though it resulted in injury, then vote no. If the majority votes yes, we will conduct a new trial to investigate the incident further." The Colonel waited for her microphone to be muted before exhaling the sigh building up within.

Even though they were given an hour to digest and cast their vote after the trial, the results were evident within the first five minutes. Out of the seventy-four thousand, five hundred and twenty-nine people on the call, seventy-four thousand, one hundred and ninety found Harvard Lewis guilty of violence. seventy-four thousand, two hundred ninety-six people voted no on the second question. The trial was complete; justice had been served.

New World, New Life

The thriving B.E.S.T. community was inspiring new wildlife, new agricultural life, and much more.

"I'm really late," Ariel blurted out to Calvin after sharing a passionate kiss.

"Late for what?" Calvin looked genuinely confused.

"I should have started menstruating weeks ago. I found an old test, and if it still works, that means I'm pregnant." Tears filled her eye ducts, her hands trembling, fearful for his reaction.

Calvin pumped his arms in the air, shaking his hips side to side, grinning ridiculously. A year ago when the world looked like it wouldn't survive the decade, the thought of having a child would have horrified him. However, now his life was amazing, and the environment B.E.S.T. created was ready to experience the joy of new life.

"Are you sure that you're happy about this?" Ariel was pacing the room, gnawing on her nails.

"Yes! This is amazing. We took every precaution and this miracle found a way to live. That's the embodiment of keeping hope alive." Calvin steaded her restless body long enough to squeeze his enthusiasm into her.

"What do you think the Colonel will say? Has anyone had a kid so far in B.E.S.T.?" Ariel spit out each question as it rose in her mind. "Do you promise to help me through this?"

"I do. I will. I think our little base community will be excited to pitch in, too. Babies are adorable and fun. You're not in this alone." He gently stroked her back as he listened to her slowly steady her breath.

"Okay. I believe you. We'll go to the medical center in Toronto, make sure everything is normal, and then talk to the Colonel. Wow, this is all so weird," Ariel said with a sigh.

She continued defining her bewilderment in her head. None of her friends had children and she hadn't spent any time around babies since she was one herself. When resources dwindled worldwide and war spread everywhere, the thought of bringing a kid into the mix was unfathomable.

This was a new world with real growth and sustainability. Maybe having a child would be considered a blessing again? Ariel grabbed onto

Calvin, pulled him as close as humanly possible, and felt joy within his embrace. Their passion created a new life.

The following morning, the lovebirds borrowed the POP to fly to Toronto where they would wait as long as required to see a physician. B.E.S.T. was still working the kinks out of their new medical system and was struggling to find qualified doctors willing to work consistent six-hour shifts. Depending on urgency, patients could wait anywhere from an hour to several days. Confirming a pregnancy wasn't dire, so they anticipated a lengthy wait. Calvin suggested baby names to pass the time.

"If it's a boy, we can name him Asher. Or maybe Jeremiah? Do you have any girl names in mind? I like Jordyn or Stephanie. Maybe Katherina? Whose last name do you want to use, 'cause that will make a difference. It shouldn't rhyme with Sinclair or Kilne. Or alliteration, like Kevin Kilne, it's too sing-songish. Don't you think so?" Calvin rambled.

"I don't care whose last name we use, but we could get married. If you want to get married. You can call the shots, Ariel. I'm a bit overly-excited and know I'd be happy if you were my wife. Do you want that?" He spewed out a string of questions too quick to be answered while Ariel breathed deeply next to him. Silence followed for a minute or two before she replied.

"I never expected to be a mom and am still trying to wrap my brain around that. I haven't even considered being a wife, or what that means in our new world." Calvin was sitting to her left; she stared straight forward, unable to look him in the eyes.

"There's no rush and no pressure. I promise. I'm here for what you decide." Calvin placed his fingertips on her chin, tilting her head towards him. "I love you and want to be with you."

"I love you, too." Ariel tried to absorb his calm confidence as she gazed into his eyes.

She felt more relaxed in the hard plastic chairs, but her body still fidgeted involuntarily. Calvin would rest his hand on her knee or arm every so often, settling her again. He tried to keep Ariel distracted by chatting about random topics, but her mind couldn't focus on his words. It jumped from worrying over how her life was about to change so drastically and pure joy that a new life was growing inside of her.

Hours dragged on and after inhaling every snack, six trips to the washroom, and playing countless games of twenty-one questions with one another, Ariel was called in. They were approaching their fourteenth hour sitting in the waiting room.

Her eyes were heavy, and Ariel almost nodded off when she heard her name echo in the room. Before she got up, Calvin placed his hands on shoulder and reassured her one final time, "No matter what, it will be okay. We're in this together." He kissed her masked face with his.

It became mandatory to wear a mask inside a hospital during the first pandemic, and now it was just common sense that was expected in the B.E.S.T. community. Doctors and nurses wore a full face shield and arm-length disposable gloves throughout the quick five-minute exam.

"Well, young lady, you were right. You are five weeks pregnant and everything is off to a great start. There are virtual classes and appointments to help guide you through until delivery. Nurse Daniel will set up the links for you and we can meet every trimester to ensure the health of you and your baby. Do you have any questions for me?" The gentleman in his mid-sixties had a sincere smile and they could feel his genuine concern.

"Wow, that is wonderful. I'm sure I'll have many questions, but right now my mind is blank." Ariel had a giddy grin and was just bursting to run into the waiting room to tell Calvin.

"Are you here alone today?" Doctor Levesque asked.

"The father is waiting outside and I can't wait to tell him." Her bouncing body made her point more evident.

"Then go ahead, just promise me you will eat well and follow the online instructional videos until we see each other again." His gentle tone and sincere concern reminded Ariel of her grandfather, who passed away due to cancer on her tenth birthday.

"I promise I will," Ariel shouted as she leapt from the table.

Without a further word, she rushed to tell Calvin the good news. Tears overwhelmed her and she couldn't speak. Luckily, the massive smile on her face told him everything. They wrapped themselves together, squeezing tighter with every tear. When they finally pulled away, he teased, "Is this your way of telling me we're going to have a baby?"

Ariel nodded her head up and down rapidly, still trying to regain her voice. The pair skipped back to the POP, hand in hand. They decided to savor one day with the news just to themselves before sharing it with the Colonel or the rest of the B.E.S.T. team at the Trenton base.

Cause for Celebration

The Colonel had just returned from visiting Rose, Matt, and the rest of the former Fort Wayne crew. In honor of their lost loved one, Amica hired an artist who specialized in memorialization to commemorate Melanie's life and sacrifice.

At Colonel Harrison's request, the artist made a concrete plaque with Melanie's name and birthdate that was secured just underneath the wall portion where the new shield connected to the original poles. She created a collage of photos from Melanie's media collection, which were framed and on display in the base's entrance way. She also etched Melanie's face into a glass cube for Rose to keep.

It was an emotional, yet necessary visit, where the Colonel not only reconfirmed that her mother's life would not be forgotten, but showed her the efforts they were making to keep Melanie alive, at least in spirit. It was heartbreaking and heartwarming, providing a sense of healing to the hardest consequence the Colonel had faced thus far. Her emotions were running wild from her visit and she immediately worried something horrible happened when Arturo tracked her down in the base's kitchen.

"I apologize for bothering you, Colonel Harrison, but Calvin and Ariel are here to see you," Arturo interrupted Amica while she was helping Royelle cut up onions and carrots for that evening's soup.

"Is everything okay?" Colonel Harrison asked her loyal assistant.

"I believe so, although I do not know the reason for their request," Arturo answered honestly.

"Oh, good, of course, no worries. Are they waiting in my office?" She replied.

"I brought them with me, or more so, they followed me back here. They're waiting in the canteen and appear to be quite anxious to speak with you," Arturo advised.

"Tell them I will be out in a moment. Thank you, Arturo." The Colonel quickly finished the carrot she was working on, washed her hands, and rushed to find out the reason for their urgency.

"Hello, Ariel and Calvin. What a pleasure to see you. You've been hopping around the country on resource gathering trips and we've hardly had a chance to connect. How is everything going?" Amica greeted the pair.

Ariel and Calvin were sitting side by side on one side of a long table; Amica took the space on the opposite side of the partian and faced them diagonally.

"It's been wonderful. We're very happy with how things are going," Ariel assured the Colonel with a toothful smile.

"Yes, we truly enjoy one another's company. Ariel has become a special part of my life, even more so with the news we're excited to share with you today," Calvin started, then paused while a loud sigh escaped. "Okay, excited and maybe a little nervous."

"I never thought this would happen," Ariel blurted out.

"Whatever it is, I'm sure we can work through it together," Amica reassured the young pair.

Calvin turned to Ariel, grasped her hand in his and gently asked, "Do you want to tell her?"

"I'm pregnant," Ariel tossed the words into the air, closed her eyes, and prayed for the right reaction.

"Wow, for real? That's amazing!" The Colonel jumped from her seat, banging her knees on the underside of the table. "Ouch! Ahh, oh who cares! You're having a baby! That's a blessing!"

"We think so," Calving announced while Ariel caught her breath.

"I wasn't sure how you'd react with another mouth to feed, especially someone who won't be able to contribute to B.E.S.T. for many years. I'm worried how I'll care for a helpless baby and still do my share," Ariel confessed.

"You won't do it alone. We're a community, and we support one another. Your focus will be on raising the next generation of B.E.S.T. team members, and we'll keep the resources flowing," Colonel Harrison reassured her treasured associate.

"I can do the supply runs solo and still be home in the evenings to help you. The Colonel is right; you're not alone," Calvin added.

Ariel gushed with tears Amica gave her a quick comforting squeeze and the happy couple left feeling relieved. The Colonel never entertained the idea of having children, but felt giddy over the thought of a baby being born in B.E.S.T. A next generation meant that there would be a future mankind. The world was not ending.

B.E.S.T. World Order

One woman believed she had a plan that would redirect the entire course of the world. At a time when hope was in short supply, she believed in herself enough to share her ideas with others. Her determination and creativity inspired a few more who passed the spark onto others, igniting a fiery passion to save the world from ultimate extinction.

A mere decade after the first unofficial meeting of B.E.S.T. at the Cabin in Smiths Falls, the old world was no longer recognizable. Within the walls of their growing community, life was genuinely peaceful and prosperous. Conflict had risen on occasion, but the majority ruled through an inclusive and accessible voting process.

Hundreds of babies were born in 2043 and that number grew into the thousands by 2053. The registered B.E.S.T. population had exceeded two million and there were now nineteen resource fulfillment centers spanning from the east to west coast. Each center had acres of farmland growing a wide range of crops, clean lakes with ample seafood, and a team to prepare and package meals for the masses. Royelle oversaw the operation as a whole to ensure everyone was giving and getting their fair share.

Their continued commitment to the four founding principles—balance, equity, stability, and teamwork—guided them through each new challenge. Dawna's team cleaned every inch of the Great Lakes, and then followed the body of water's natural flow, cleaning every feeder river and stream. They were currently working on the southern end of Hudson Bay, and planned on continuing their clean up towards the east. A separate crew with a slightly smaller filtration system was running it through lakes in the north-est.

The B.E.S.T. wall of recyclables had now been extended from the Atlantic Ocean to the Pacific Ocean, jetting through Minnisota, all the way to Washington. They tragically lost one construction employee in an accident where a cable snapped, dropping a section of the wall directly on top of him, reinforcing an emphasis on ensuring everyone's safety.

There were no further attacks from the south, and the outside world remained a mystery to most of those who lived within the

B.E.S.T.

B.E.S.T. community walls. In the first ten years, there had only been four murders on record, a shockingly low statistic for a population well into the millions. Harvard's wife was the first, followed by two domestic violence situations involving kitchen knives where the abuser was immediately convicted and evicted from B.E.S.T.

The third was a neighborly dispute that escalated slowly over several years. In a heated argument, one man struck another with a shovel, cracking his skull. The assailant was charged, tried, and found guilty, resulting in expulsion. Guns had been confiscated over the years, but with the exception of Harvard's, all were found before being fired.

Food, clean water, and fresh air were now in ample supply within the B.E.S.T. walls and no one wanted to risk being kicked out. They graciously followed the relatively easy rules, established to guide their new country in a better direction. Everyone contributed and benefited from one another's hard work, so there wasn't any reason to cause conflict.

The Colonel held herself solely responsible for the overall safety of everyone with the B.E.S.T. borders, and had a secret control room where she monitored threats from the outside world. She also had eight Major Security Officers, Rose, Matt, Josée, Tamika, Tobin, Bella, Jarrod, and Antonio, who were spread out throughout the country, keeping an eye on the border wall.

Amica was unable to find out how the people she left in the 'Badlands' of Australia turned out, since there had been no communication to anyone in North America coming from the shrinking continent. There were also no news alerts from the Eastern Hemisphere coming across their wristbands. If people still existed on the other side of the world, no one was trying to contact anyone within B.E.S.T.

The southern side of the continent B.E.S.T. shared with rebel masses wasn't as quiet. Reuter reports sent from journalists who chose not to stay within the walls of B.E.S.T. kept the Colonel informed of any pending danger. Weekly reports of mass shootings and violent robberies were summarized in bullet points, as there were far too many to provide any significant detail.

Freedom Fighters Rage War & Hundreds Die.

Violence and the associated death toll that has accompanied it continues to skyrocket in the former NSC and the lawless remains of N.U.R. without any signs of decline.

Here are the tragic events for the week of April third, 2053.

- *A gang-style mass shooting in Utah claimed the lives of over one hundred, when seventeen armed men took over an operational hospital. They are now holding four doctors and six nurses hostage.*

- *A mass shooting at a local Kentucky Market took the lives of twenty-four individuals, ranging from age three to forty-seven.*

- *A mass shooting at an abandoned hotel in Colorado claimed the lives of thirty-one people.*

- *Sixteen Texans, from three separate families, were killed today when invaders forcibly took over their joint residents.*

- *Four women between the ages of seventeen and twenty-eight were raped and murdered, left on the Vegas Strip to die.*

- *Two grocery store clerks and nine customers were killed in Kansas today when four former Kansas City Royals took over the store swinging baseball bats and heavy chains.*

- *Wildfires took the lives of hundreds in California.*

- *A tropical storm wiped out the coast of North Carolina, killing thousands.*

Every report from the outside made Amica grateful she acted when she did, especially insisting on a border in spite of its past unpopularity. Evil, or greater environmental catastrophes, would have made its way north and destroyed any chance of rebuilding.

On the other side of the rubber tires and plastic poles divide was pending death. As the situation south of B.E.S.T. became more dire, internal warfare broke out and it was every man for themselves. Their lack of unity and constant chaos was exactly what the Colonel needed to protect the flourishing B.E.S.T. world from being infiltrated. Threats fell as quickly as they rose.

A few years prior, a dirty dozen-style gang rose in Texas and took credit for killing thousands of Americans over a four-month period. They gained more members as they headed through New Mexico into Colorado. The B.E.S.T. team was finishing the wall section in Montana when Colonel Harrison received a report that the gang had at least three dozen members and went on a shooting spree in Wyoming.

They were growing, had exerted their control over the south, and were rapidly heading north. The Colonel was on higher alert until an even larger gang was formed that eventually wiped out the first. The group of fifty that overpowered the original threat moved south-west, and ended up setting up home in Missouri.

Violence and mass murders were the only topic that arose from below, and Amica tracked each incident on an old 3-D globe. She exhaled relief at the end of each day, knowing that no one was currently attempting to use deadly force to destroy B.E.S.T. Although it took a team of hundreds, and thousands of willing people to fix the world, Amica couldn't help but feel responsible for every life that signed the B.E.S.T contract.

Ideally, humanity wouldn't wait until the world had spiraled completely out of control to try to save it, but humans are far from ideal. It took an inevitable threat of no possible future to finally wake people up enough to be willing to change their ways. The actual work required to save our earth was never the issue; people had to feel the fear of utter extinction to finally do something about it.

If you give the world your best, it will give you its best.